COOKIE FAMOUS

A FAMOUS ROMANCE NOVEL

CALLIE CHASE

Cover design by Regina Wamba
ISBN 978-1-950348-37-4

COOKIE FAMOUS

CALLIE CHASE

This book is dedicated with love and gratitude to the mothers and mother figures of all varieties—both here and departed. Your love lives on in all we dream, create, and are.

And to the lost relationships. The ones who got away. The crushes we never kissed. The loves we couldn't keep forever. Have a cookie and savor the sweetness of the stories past and yet to come.

ONE

"These cookies are so perfect!" Nicolette Hayes said, her voice sweet with delight. "You beauties are going to be *famous!*"

Just as she said that, she knocked one cookie off the perfectly staged display she'd been photographing. The complicated frosted confection shattered into a dozen pieces on the floor of the bakery kitchen.

"Well," she muttered, giggling at the mess, "not today. But maybe someday."

Nicolette was the baker, the frosting artist, and the cleaner of after-baking messes. Cookies were her life, and this particular batch—these held the keys to her future.

Even under the film of flour that dusted Nic's touchscreen her work looked vibrant, adorable, and delicious. She looked over the dozens of pictures she'd taken with her smartphone. Row after row of sugar cookies had been piped to looked like spaceships. Her baked works of art practically leapt from the screen. The multi-colored macaron unicorns made her smile, even though when she'd been bent over decorating them, pastry bag in hand, she'd sweated over every detail. She grinned at the crown jewel of her cookie portfolio, her shortbread kraken, its buttery tentacles breaking a gingerbread ship to crumbs.

"Nic, are you still here?" Her boss's voice drifted into the kitchen.

Nicolette startled, her surroundings snapping back into sharp focus. Covered in flour and icing, Nicolette had only meant to take a short break before setting the kitchen to rights and heading home. She'd been at work since four a.m., decorating the literary-themed cookies for an event. Now it was nearly dark. She was so tired she practically swayed on her feet as she realized just how late it was.

"Sorry, Luz!" Nic said, quickly pocketing her phone. "Got distracted. I'll clean up right now!"

Luz, her boss and mentor, walked over to Nic and leaned against the counter next to her. "Distracted?" she asked with a grin, used to her star baker being exactly that.

Nicolette nodded, biting her lip. "Yes, I was taking some pictures of the cookies I made for the book launch. The designs are so perfect..." Nic flushed even as she complimented her own work. "Well, you know what I mean... They are freaking adorable, right?"

Luz gave Nic a wry smile. "You don't need to apologize for loving your work. You're the best this bakery has ever had. And yes..." Luz shook her head as she looked over the perfectly iced unicorns. "These are freaking adorable!"

"So you see how I lost track of time taking pictures!"

Luz grew serious as she looked her employee in the eye. "Does this have anything to do with the proposal for the comic convention?"

Nic dropped her eyes to the floor as she silently counted the number of days until the proposal was due. "Blue Hippo Animation is going to have one of the biggest booths at the fan event this year. If they pick me to make their cookies..."

Nicolette didn't have to explain. The exposure to thousands—tens of thousands—of fans, maybe more, not to mention all the other booths and business at the convention... If Nic's portfolio was picked, she could launch herself as a serious cookie artist. She could open her own bakery. She could...well, the dreams she had were big, but right now, the biggest star in her sky was owning a bakery. *Her* bakery. She knew what she would call it. Cookie Spectacle—a nod to the signature cat-eye glasses she wore whenever she didn't have her contacts in. Which was almost all the time.

Nic had spent countless hours daydreaming, doodling images of the storefront, her future logos... She could only imagine someday having a whole bakery decorated in her signature style of art. With her cookies for sale. She loved making everything she made for Bread-n-Batter—in fact, she probably owed her entire career to Luz—but Nicolette knew the only way she could devote all of her artistic talent to her work was... if she could devote all of her artistic talent to her work. And that meant being her own boss. Eventually.

"So," Luz nudged, looking at Nic with concern etched on her face. "You're just taking pictures today? Why haven't you turned the proposal in yet? Isn't it due like, soon?"

Nicolette looked at her boss, wrinkling her brow in surprise. "How did you...?"

Luz's affection-filled laugh carried through the warm kitchen. "Oh, honey. I've known you for five years. I know how that mind works."

Luz stood in front of Nicolette and reached for her hands.

"You're ready, love. You know that. You're just worried about me and Alfonso. Which is ridiculous. If you get the opportunity of a lifetime, you need to know the people who really love you will be behind you all the way."

Nic swallowed her response—which was going to be something sappy and covered in tears.

Luz continued, waving her arm around the kitchen, "We'll be just fine. Bakers come and go, but friends..." She grinned at Nic. "Now that's a rare gift."

Luz paused to let the sincerity of her words settle before teasing Nic with a nudge to the ribs. "We'll miss you and your weird aprons though."

Nicolette glanced down at her now-dirty apron. She could barely make out the frogs riding motorcycles through the haze of flour and stains from the coloring she'd used for the icing. Nic grinned—she did have eclectic taste. But that was what made her such a detail-oriented artist. Who better to paint sunglasses on narwhal-shaped shortbread than someone who brought whimsy into the everyday?

Luz smiled at Nic, sincerity infused in every encouraging word. "Turn in that proposal. You show Blue Hippo what you're made of! We'll support you every step of the way."

Nicolette nodded. "Thank you," she whispered.

Luz waved her away. "Please, or I'll start crying. Turn in the proposal *now*, before you miss your chance. And then clean this kitchen!"

Nicolette saluted, causing Luz to chuckle as she left the kitchen.

Grabbing a rag from the disinfectant bucket, Nicolette started wiping down the flour-crusted counters, humming under her breath. She wasn't going to submit the proposal from her smartphone. She'd wait until she got home, could make sure the pictures and the bio she'd written were absolutely perfect, and then...tonight...

A sudden jingle from her pocket gave her pause. There was only one notification that made that sound. That was the tone she'd set up for Rio, her famous hockey-playing brother.

He was not particularly good at keeping in touch, so she'd set her phone to alert her whenever he did something newsworthy.

She dried her hands on a clean-ish part of her frog apron and retrieved her phone from her pocket. A grin lit up her face as she wondered if this was a real news story, or if this was a social media hit. Knowing Rio, Nic guessed her brother had graced some red carpet event last night, the hottie-of-the-week plastered against his $5,000 suit, and the photo had just hit the afternoon's entertainment blogs.

But Nicolette's mirth soon caught in her throat as a news flash filled her phone screen.

BUS CARRYING INDIANAPOLIS GUARDIANS CRASHES

Nicolette cried out as she clicked to expand the article. Her eyes touched on the highlights of the story, each detail adding to her panic: *extent of injuries unknown, players taken to area hospitals, families notified.* And there, at the end, was a list of names of players on the bus.

For just a moment, idiotic hope flared. Maybe her brother wasn't on that bus. Maybe he'd been with that hottie and had slept in and was now reading the news with the same mounting horror that she was feeling.

But then the lights of the bakery seemed to dim along with Nic's hope as she saw her brother's name on the list of Guardians players on the bus: *Rio Hayes.*

Her legs felt weak and she heard her sobs, gut-deep and hoarse, as if from a distance. With a shaking finger, she closed the news article and pulled up the dial pad on her phone. Nicolette closed her eyes and waited.

Her father answered immediately. "Nic!" He sounded wrecked, and Nicolette's heart cracked at the raw emotion in her dad's voice.

"Daddy?" she managed through her tears. "What's happened?"

~

10:37 P.M. It was an hour later in Chicago than it was in Denver. Nicolette had never hated the difference in times zones between her and her father more than she did right now. She'd been on the phone with him constantly since Luz had dropped her off at her apartment. Her boss had offered to stay with her, but Nicolette's roommate, Rhoslyn, had rushed home too and promised to smother Nic with good food and support. Luz had left Nicolette with a crushing hug and instructions to keep her updated, and to absolutely not come into work until she knew what was happening back at home.

Nicolette had only been able to nod through her tears.

Nic's roommate and dear friend Rhoslyn had lived up to her word. With the application of tissues, tea, and some much-needed dinner, she'd managed to calm Nicolette to something just short of hysterical.

Rhoslyn tried to pour Nic another cup of tea. "Drink, sweetie." Rhoslyn filled the Jane Austen–inspired teacup that she saved for special occasions, or in this case, heady emergencies. "This is a new blend I'm trying out. It's called 'Bloom Where You're Planted.'"

Nic looked quizzically at her roommate.

"It's a special blend of serene, calming flowers and fruity notes. No caffeine." Rhoslyn filled the delicate china cup. "Hydration is the best thing you can do right now. You'll wear yourself out if you cry all night, and that won't help anyone."

Nicolette declined the tea, although she knew that would likely break Rhoslyn's heart. The woman was Denver's only tea sommelier and had practically made it her life's mission to cure anything that ailed anyone through a custom blend of tea, listening, and love. But Nic felt like she was swimming in tea and tears. She passed on the cup, though she took Rhoslyn's advice and made herself calm down. But not because she cared if she made herself sick. Because she had to be strong for her dad. He didn't have anyone else. He'd never quite recovered from her mother's death. Nicolette couldn't imagine what the stress of knowing Rio might be hurt was doing to him.

Rhoslyn watched Nic while Nic watched the sports news network, hoping for faster updates on the story than she was getting on her phone. When the caller ID popped up with her dad's name yet again, Nicolette answered the call immediately and put it on speakerphone.

"A representative from the team just called," her dad, Keith, said without even a hello, his voice reedy and strained.

Rhoslyn squeezed Nicolette's hand.

"They brought Rio here to Chicago."

Nicolette's tension eased a fraction. "That's good, Dad. You can be with him."

"Yeah..." He trailed off. "Listen, they aren't really telling me anything else. I think... Kiddo, I think you should come home."

RHOSLYN PULLED her hatchback up to the curb, the pre-dawn light just touching her worried face. "Are you going to be okay flying?" she asked.

Nicolette bit her lip to keep fresh tears from escaping. "I will be. I'm okay," she said, trying to focus on what would get her through these next few hours—being strong for her dad and for Rio.

Rhoslyn nodded, and they got out of the car. Together they

pulled a single suitcase from the trunk.

Rhoslyn gripped Nicolette in a crushing hug. "Let me know when you get there."

Nicolette nodded. "I promise," she said.

In a daze, Nicolette checked her luggage and wandered through security. She barely knew what was happening as she got on the plane. She found her seat and dropped into it, happy to be able to close her eyes and hopefully not think for the better part of the next few hours. She doubted she'd be able to rest, but the quiet would do her mind good.

A middle-aged man in a business suit plunked down next to her and pulled a newspaper from his bag. Splashed across the front page was a picture of the bus crash, the grainy ink not obscuring the seriousness of the wreckage.

Nicolette turned away, a hand over her mouth to keep from crying out.

She tried to turn her thoughts to something, anything, to keep from imagining what might be happening to Rio.

She had sent Luz a text, and her boss had immediately answered, telling her that her job would be available whenever Nicolette could come back. But Nicolette knew the schedule. The bakery had events lined up, and she wouldn't be there to help, and...

Worrying about work wasn't helping keep her emotions in check and stop *worrying*. Taking a deep breath, Nicolette curled herself into the window seat, and just tried to make it through the flight.

She must have dozed at some point, because Nicolette startled awake as the plane bumped through its landing. She deplaned in a sleepy daze and followed the other passengers as they wandered through the deserted airport to the baggage claim. Her dad had promised he would arrange a ride for her, so she kept her phone close, waiting for details.

As she waited in the sea of anonymous people, she closed her eyes. Exhaustion warred with a hyper alertness, and her insides felt scrambled. She knew she must look terrible, her eyes swollen from crying and her hair a forgotten concern. She'd literally dressed in the dark.

Nicolette forced her eyes open and was pleasantly surprised to see her suitcase cruising toward her on the belt. The magenta and lime plaid was easy to spot in the sea of black.

She muscled her way through a group of passengers and grabbed for her bag. But it was heavy—she hadn't known how long she'd be staying so she'd packed a lot—and it was partially trapped under someone else's heavy-looking duffel. As she grappled with the handle, anger fought with the sadness that had weighed down her soul. She tried not to cry out in frustration, but she could have used a little, teeny-tiny break. She would be *damned* if she would be defeated by a suitcase. Not at a time like this.

But then, before Nic could scramble along the conveyor and chase after her bag, she got more than a teeny-tiny break. Like an angel reaching down from heaven, an arm reached past her and easily pulled the suitcase from the belt.

Brushing her hair back from her face, Nicolette turned to thank her savior. And stopped. And stared. And *stared*.

Matthew Collins was standing before her, holding her suitcase in his capable hands.

Matthew. Fucking. Collins.

The object of the biggest, most ridiculous, absolute failure of a crush of her entire life.

He was here. And he looked more gorgeous than anyone had the right to at five in the morning.

"Matthew?" she exclaimed, her crying-sore voice sounding like a frog croaking.

She hadn't seen Matthew except in her sweaty, lust-filled dreams since she'd moved to Denver. Memories came flooding back to Nic—the hours, no, years—at the hockey rink watching Rio and Matthew run drills on the ice. The way at age eight Matthew had seemed so solid, so serious, especially about hockey, always showing up at their house at least an hour before practice to talk hockey before hitching a ride to the rink. The way his chin even at fourteen was strong and stubbled with light blond hairs. The way he seemed to notice when she watched him skate, his head turning slightly as he spun past her in the cold practice arena. The way at seventeen his entire body seemed to hold his passions in check, his sweetness revealed in the tiniest gestures and looks. Things only Nic seemed to notice about the gentle, hulking giant.

His dark blue eyes had always held storms of emotion, and for as long as Nic lived, there would be no blue that she could mix or make that could compare to the natural beauty this man had been endowed with. And now those blue eyes stared down at her in a fury.

The shock and excitement that filled Nic at seeing Matthew was a welcome change from her despair, and she threw her arms around him without thinking. As soon as her hands laced behind his back, and the very grown-up body of the boy she'd loved so much touched hers, Nic nearly forgot the reason she was here. The airport full of weary strangers, the mangled bus...the future of the brother she loved and whose entire childhood was intricately woven with the man whom she was holding now... All that faded as Nic for just a moment let herself go back to that magical, happy place where Matthew was her crush and her hero and where Rio and Matthew and their third buddy, Austin, were the unstoppable forces that gave her childhood direction.

Larger than life, bigger than dreams. Nic embraced

Matthew like she was holding on to the past and was doing her best to keep it safe.

Only Matthew didn't seem to welcome the memories and the past. He noticeably stiffened in her hold and pulled back slightly. Nic was shaken from her dreamy state by his tension. She dropped her arms and wrapped them around herself. Then she laughed—the sound literally her embarrassment come to life. "Uh, sorry! It's been a crazy night, you know? It's just soooo good to see you again!"

Matthew's expression darkened as if she'd just told him he had shit on his shoes and salad in his teeth.

Okay, she thought, *this is odd.* She wondered if maybe his reaction had to do with what he knew about Rio. She hadn't even had time to check her phone for more updates. "I'm so worried," she admitted. She looked at him hopefully. "Have you seen him?" she asked.

Matthew's face was blank. He set her suitcase down on its wheels and roughly grabbed the handle. He wore a thick down jacket but Nic could tell his arms were as strong as they'd ever been by how easily he hefted the weight of her things.

"No," Matthew finally said, his voice tumbling out low and granite-hard. That gorgeous chin was set at an angry angle, the light stubble of his beard looking harsher than it did in Nic's memories...and fantasies. "I'm only here as a favor," he gritted out. "Let's go."

Without waiting for Nicolette's response, Matthew turned and strode away, his cold words freezing Nicolette's tears.

～

JUST A FEW HOURS AGO, the phone ringing at midnight had set cold fear trickling down Matthew's spine. He'd been slightly relieved when it had been Austin Ames, his best friend.

"You awake?" Austin's voice had been strained, putting Matthew on alert again.

"I am now. What is it?" Matthew demanded, flipping back the covers. "What's wrong?"

Austin took a shaky breath. "There's been an accident. Rio's team's bus crashed."

The information froze Matthew in place. Rio. When was the last time he and Austin had spoken about the man who had once been like a brother to him? When was the last time he even let himself think about Rio fucking Hayes?

"Okay," Matthew said, rubbing his unshaven jaw. "I'm sorry to hear that." He forced out a polite response—the bare minimum he could manage for a guy like fucking Hayes. "What's that got to do with me?" he finally asked.

"I'm at the hospital with Keith," Austin said, as though that explained everything.

Rio's dad. Another person Matthew had banished from his thoughts. Again, Matthew wondered what any of this had to do with him.

"Nicolette is flying into Midway," Austin continued. "I need you to pick her up."

Nicolette Hayes. Now that name was a blast from the past. Rio's geeked-out little sister. The girl couldn't have been more opposite from the trio of athletes who seemed to take up every room of the Hayes house while they were growing up. Matthew tugged a hand through his hair as he thought back to Rio's little sister. She'd been adorable—a word he would never have used then, but which definitely fit now, looking back. Always sketching and shoving her funky glasses up on her nose, Nic seemed to be in the background of nearly every memory he had of his childhood. At least the parts off the ice. Of the Hayes family, whom he'd blocked from his mind for many reasons, Nic was the only one not tainted with some kind of anger, guilt.

When his parents' lives went to shit, which seemed to start when he was about eight and didn't end until he finally stopped speaking to them, Nic had been the one who helped pitch in and watch his little sister, Shelby. While his younger brother, Jackson, was off feeling up the neighborhood girls in garages and on the playground, Nic had taken little Shelby in hand and babysat her at the hockey rink. They'd spend hours together waiting for Rio's parents to bring them all home again—because Matthew's parents couldn't be bothered with anything so mundane as taking kids to practice. At least Matthew had had hockey. Shelby only had Nic.

"Matthew?" Austin demanded. "Are you there? Nic's on a plane, man. She can't come home to this and jump in a rideshare at five in the morning. You got this?"

Matthew wasn't even sure he'd recognize Nicolette when he saw her. It had been years...a lot of years since the last time he'd spoken to Rio. He'd never forget the look on Nic's face when he'd stormed out of the Hayes house for the last time. So many times he'd seen her watching him, something hidden behind those glasses and the small curve of her smile. But that day, the day that would end his connection to everything he loved forever, Nic's face looked shattered. Sad. Who would grown-up Nicolette be?

Doesn't fucking matter, he thought with irritation, as he threw his flannel pajama pants in a heap on the floor. *She's part of the past, she's part of Rio, and so to me, she's fucking history.*

But because Matthew couldn't say no to Austin, he'd gotten in his car in the middle of the damn night to drive to the airport, trying to tame his churning brain.

God, this was bullshit. He couldn't believe he would do this—even for Nicolette. Because behind all of this was *Rio*. No doubt they'd give that asshole a few stitches and he'd leave the hospital via a red carpet. Five models with champagne would appear so that Rio could mug for the press like the diva he was. If anything, this little bus accident would just fuel Rio's legendary reputation.

Matthew ground his teeth. This shouldn't be his problem. He'd cut off contact with Rio ten years ago. After Matthew had been forced to give up hockey, maintaining a friendship with Rio would have been like chewing glass. Protecting himself when no one else cared had meant he'd had to make painful sacrifices.

Not that Rio had mourned their friendship. Just like everyone else, he hadn't seemed to care much what happened after Matthew dropped out of sight. Matthew's memories and emotions whipped back and forth as he drove through the dim Chicago dawn. And Nicolette...the accident must have been serious if Nic was on a red-eye. That gave Matthew a moment's pause. Rio had always been Nic's world—that much had been obvious. She must be terrified and stressed out. Matthew knew this wasn't the first serious loss the Hayes family had suffered. But Matthew couldn't allow himself to think about that. About his former best friend and his life. Not when that asshole had cost Matthew everything.

But Matthew wasn't completely heartless. Nic wasn't guilty of anything—other than being the sister of the biggest jagoff in the history of hockey. He'd agree to do what Austin asked. He'd pick up Rio's kid sister and then that would be it.

This determination had propelled him into the airport to the baggage claim.

Where all of his convictions were shanghaied and held at gunpoint.

Nicolette Hayes was instantly recognizable. Her brownish-red hair floated around her head in a messy cloud, and her green eyes were swollen from crying. Everything on her looked mismatched and wrinkled. She was not wearing makeup, and her skin was blotchy.

Matthew stopped short just inside the door. This was definitely the dorky girl he remembered, all bright colors and awkwardness.

But as Matthew continued to stare, he saw all the subtle changes that ten years made. She was taller, and her curves were fuller and softer. She was still quirky but carried herself with a confidence that made her fascinating. And sexy.

Matthew's skin tightened as he realized where his mind was taking him.

"No," he whispered. He reminded himself why he was here. Nicolette was Rio's sister. Nothing could change that, no matter how much she'd grown up.

He'd approached as she'd struggled with her suitcase, planning to grab the bag and get back to the car with minimal conversation.

And then she'd hugged him. The suitcase had blocked most of any real physical contact, but her soft hair had brushed his jaw. A subtle scent of something sweet tempted his nose. Matthew's eyes drifted shut for just a moment, imagining that scent wrapping around him, following him to his home, to his bed... *What the actual fuck?*

He practically dragged Nicolette out of the airport after that, trying to escape the rush of memories and the intoxicating fragrance of *her*. But there was no relief to be had. It was too cold to open the windows, and Nic's presence infused his car with notes of vanilla and cake. The awareness of her warm body just across the console was a next-level distraction, and Matthew almost missed the exit to get onto the highway as he pulled out of the airport.

Instead of the contemplative silence he'd hoped she would

want, Nicolette started chatting immediately.

"God, it's been so long, Matthew," she said, a note in her voice that he couldn't quite decipher.

He could see her gaze fixed on him out of the corner of his eye. She was watching him. Again. Like she'd always seemed to do. But instead of making him uncomfortable, Matthew found himself relaxing in spite of himself. It was like they had this familiar connection and even though a decade had passed, they slid right back into their old roles.

"How's Shelby?" Nicolette asked. "I remember babysitting her so many times. All those practices." A grin lit up Nic's words. These were fond memories. For her. "She must be in college by now?" Nic asked.

"She's fine," Matthew said. "She's studying business at Holy Mother."

"That's great!" Nicolette gushed. "Your parents must be so proud."

Matthew grunted, hoping she would take the hint that he really wasn't interested in catching up. This entire scene was agony—her scent, her musical voice, the warm zing of his blood in his veins. Her connection to his past and everything that had mattered. It was all too dangerous, threatening to peel back too much of his armor.

"What about Jackson?" Nicolette continued blithely.

"We're fine," Matthew growled. "My sister is fine, my brother is fine. That's the last decade in a nutshell, okay?"

Finally the silence descended. He threw a glance Nicolette's way and saw her biting her lower lip, hugging her arms with white-knuckled hands.

God, he was such an asshole. She was just trying to be nice. She was doing what old friends did. What normal, non-ragey, non-damaged people who hadn't seen each other in forever did.

But nice and normal were not in Matthew's vocabulary, especially when it came to his family. His life. Fucking Rio.

But Nicolette couldn't know that. He hoped like hell she didn't know.

"Uh, so where am I taking you?" Matthew asked, trying to imbue some softness into his voice. He couldn't apologize, but he could try to be nicer. Just a little. Just for Nic.

"Chicago Medical Center," she answered quietly.

Matthew's hackles rose again. Damn it, this was turning out to be just a treat of a day. Not only did he have to rehash his past, but Chicago Medical Center would take him in the exact opposite direction of where he needed to be. He'd scheduled an on-site inspection on a commercial building in Ukrainian Village for first thing in the morning and at this rate, he would be lucky to get back home in time to shower, change, and reach the site for the 7:00 a.m. appointment.

A historic neighborhood social club was for sale—it was too small to turn into condos, but the space had been zoned for mixed use. Matthew had been contemplating actually buying property for once. He worked as a commercial real estate agent and had brokered many deals and he'd finally saved up enough for a down payment on a place he could rent out for income. He'd gotten the scoop on the place from a buddy who was in construction. It was still in the demolition phase, but the flipper who'd bought it wanted to put feelers out, hoping to find an interested buyer before they got too far into the renovation. His appointment to see the place had required scheduling magic—and at this rate, he'd be lucky if he was fashionably late.

The tap-tapping of Nicolette's fingers on the console stopped Matthew's descent into full-on grump. She jiggled her leg in time with the silent rhythm in her head, her eyes darting to keep up with the cars zipping by them. Her nerves were nearly palpable, and he was tempted to reach over and rest a comforting hand on her knee.

"Are you married?" she suddenly blurted. "Any kids?"

"Nope," Matthew intoned, refusing to elaborate into the silence his answer left. His personal life was not up for examination. Especially not with this woman. Rio's artsy little sis was filling the SUV with emotions and memories of the past, but also with a new, uncomfortable awareness. He felt the weight of her as she watched him drive. She seemed completely oblivious to the fact that she was turned slightly in her seat, staring at him. And like it had for so many years when they were kids, her steady presence and quiet understanding seemed to bring him calm. Back to center. Except this—this was different. Now when he chanced a peek at her from the corner of his eye, he *saw* her. The fullness of her lower lip as she traced the tip of her tongue along its edge. The way her soft layers whooshed against the wool of her coat when she fluffed out her hair. The peek of her thighs, covered in patterned tights, under the unseasonably short skirt she wore.

The seesaw of desire and the urge to run as far away from her as possible was making him dizzy.

"What do you do for a living?" she barged on, unaware of his tightening jaw.

"Real estate," he said, trying to focus on the traffic instead of her delicate hands. She had short, unpainted nails, and wore a few slender rings. Her ring finger was bare. As if that was an important detail.

Nicolette nodded like he'd just given her an in-depth biography and pushed her glasses up on her nose. They were purple tortoiseshell and made her expressive eyes pop.

Shit. No matter how he wanted to stay in his righteous silence, every detail of Nicolette Hayes seemed to beg for his attention. He tried to shift his focus back to traffic.

"Do you still play hockey?" she asked.

Matthew stiffened. He could see her little smile out of the corner of his eye, and he knew exactly what she was remembering. Him, Rio, and Austin mucking around at practices or dominating on the ice at games. All those summers spent at Rio's house, feeling like he was a part of a family, a home. And Nicolette, the funny little shadow, always angling to be in the room with her big brother and his two best friends.

And she was still angling, wanting to open up that locked room in his heart, threatening bringing back all that joy and the devastation.

"No" was all he said, practically choking on the sudden sorrow that her simple question had stirred in him.

This whole situation was fucked.

As they approached the hospital, Nicolette grew quiet, the only sound from her side of the car her soft, sad-sounding breaths.

Matthew hated how relieved he was that this drive was almost over. This entire night would become just a blip in his otherwise ordered life. All the memories would be stuffed back down where they belonged, and Matthew would go back to his work. These days work was the only thing he had, and he wouldn't let anything—or anyone—stop him from success. Not this time.

And he would absolutely not think any more about Nicolette.

"Do you know anything?" she asked, her voice strained. "About Rio's condition. Did Austin tell you anything?"

"Just that he was in the crash," Matthew said, and suddenly his mouth started running. "I wouldn't worry too much. I'm sure he's fine. Right about now he's convinced some nurse to make out with him and another to sneak him an Instagram-worthy cheeseburger. Gotta get those likes, after all."

They pulled into the passenger loading zone of the hospital, and Matthew finally looked at Nicolette. Hurt was etched deeply on her face, and worse, tears had begun to slip out from under her glasses.

Something tightened in Matthew's chest, and he opened his mouth to offer soothing words. He could wrap his arms around her, too. Be an anchor as she let go of that worry. It would be so easy.

No. This was not his responsibility. She was not his, in any sense. He'd relinquished rights to her and her family long ago. Not just relinquished. Extinguished.

Without waiting to see if she would follow, Matthew got out of the car and retrieved her suitcase from the back and wheeled it to the curb.

Nicolette climbed slowly and stiffly from the car, like her limbs weren't working properly. She grabbed her suitcase handle, staring at the ridiculous pattern for a few moments. It looked like she was trying to look at anything but him.

"Thank you," she said, her voice surprisingly even after that brief show of tears. "For the ride."

"Sure," he answered easily.

Nicolette finally looked up at him, her green eyes startlingly bright in the new morning light.

"Are you coming in?" she asked.

He didn't understand the hope in her expression. He thought he'd made it clear.

"No," he said, not bothering to offer any explanation. "But good luck."

Matthew turned and strode back to his car, all too aware that Nicolette was still standing on the curb watching him go.

Pulling away, he put the hospital in his rearview mirror, trying hard to ignore the whisper of *coward* that got louder the farther he drove.

TWO

Nicolette hadn't slept in twenty-four hours. Other than a couple minutes of fitful, eyes-closed "rest" on the plane, she'd been awake since she'd started the unicorn cookies in the wee hours yesterday at Bread-n-Batter. What a difference a day made. Yesterday, Nic had been consumed with concerns about the Blue Hippo proposal—how her applying would make Luz feel...and what her chances of making it really were.

Today, her brother was in this hospital. She had no idea what condition he was in, and all she knew was that her father was hurting, her brother was in trouble, and Blue Hippo seemed like a childish dream compared to the very tragic realities facing her family.

But for some reason, it was her disappointment in Matthew Collins that was pushing her over the edge.

Her memories of him had been gilt-edged. Always the tallest of the three boys, he was also the quietest and the hardest working. He never seemed to want to go home, so her parents let him hang around. He'd always been the helper, the reliable and steady one. And to see him play hockey...all that athleticism and passion. Quiet, strong, funny, but never the center of attention. Never the guy who sought out the spot-light. Rio hadn't been that guy either, but somehow with his darker features and his more obvious natural talent, Rio had ended up front and center. Nic adored her brother, always had, but baby Nicolette had thought Matthew...Matthew was the perfect man.

Until today. The all-grown-up man who'd met her at baggage claim was nothing like the boy she remembered. His ocean-dark eyes no longer glittered with innocence and sweet-ness. There was something angry there now, something that Nic didn't recognize and didn't understand. The playfulness of his smile had been replaced by the hard set of his stubbled chin and lips—though still gorgeous and full—that were set to a permanent sulk. There was no denying who Matthew had become. He was cold and *mean*. Speaking in stiff, one-word sentences, he'd barely looked at her. They'd grown up together, their lives intertwining until it seemed impossible to separate Matthew from even a single childhood memory, but yet he'd treated her like a stranger. An unwelcome imposition. Even all those years ago when Nic hovered in the shadows, she'd had the sense that she belonged there. That in a way, she was welcome in their wild, rambunctious group. This Matthew clearly wanted to put as much distance between them as possible.

Even worse were the things he'd said about Rio. It was as if there was nothing to be worried about. As if he didn't even care that his oldest, closest friend was lying in who knew what condition, suffering in untold ways alone. What had happened to the enormous sweetheart whose face filled Nic's every waking thought and sleeping dreams?

That man she saw today wasn't the Matthew she'd fanta-sized about for years. He was a flimsy paper cutout, superficial and weak. And the disappointment was breaking Nicolette's already fragile heart.

"Whatever." Nicolette stood on the curb outside the hospital entrance and straightened her shoulders. She couldn't waste time on him if he couldn't be bothered to care about them. He'd picked her up and saved her the trouble of finding a rideshare in the wee hours of the morning. She had to put him out of her mind and focus on the real reason she was home— Rio. And her dad.

Even still, as she shivered in the chilly dawn air, she couldn't help but wonder why. What could have happened to turn such a soft heart so hard? She had no excuses, no insight, so she fell back on the only possible excuse she could think of. "He's just an asshole," she reminded herself. "I'll never know why or how, it's just better to forget him."

But she couldn't help wondering, questioning exactly what had happened to him. The Matthew of her memories couldn't have just been a fabrication of a star-struck teen mind. He had been every bit of everything that she'd believed he was...wasn't he?

She tried to remember that last year. She'd been fifteen— peak awkwardness—and more aware of Matthew than ever. At nineteen, he'd begun to really fill out, his hockey obsession contributing to muscles in delightful places. As ever, Rio, Matthew, and Austin were thick as thieves. Hockey and girls and video games were all they cared about, and the future looked bright.

And then Matthew just disappeared. He stopped coming to the house. He even stopped playing hockey. Nicolette had known that something must have been terribly wrong for Matthew to drop hockey, but no one ever said anything. Her brother would just shrug and say that Matthew had made his choice. Austin was even more close-lipped. In an instant, it was like Matthew Collins had never even existed. The void he left in their house had never quite been filled, but not long after Matthew disappeared, the trio would have broken up anyway. Rio was off to his pro hockey career and Austin, who was never really destined for more than an amateur career, went to work at his mom's diner.

The Hayes house was suddenly emptier than ever, every room haunted by the ghosts of the boys who'd given it life. But especially by the one boy who'd given Nic chills even outside of the rink.

A vibration in her pocket made Nicolette jump, and she pulled her phone free.

It was a text from Rhoslyn.

ARE YOU OK WHAT'S GOING ON I AM SO WORRIED CALL ME ASAP!!!!!

Nicolette had to smile at her friend's lack of punctuation... while at the same time she overused it. Nic walked a little closer to the entrance of the hospital and dialed her roommate.

"Woman!" Rhoslyn shouted into the phone. "Why didn't you call me as soon as you landed? I haven't been able to sleep!"

"I'm sorry, Rhoslyn. It's just...it's been a crazy night." Nic's heart didn't know which to feel first—sadness, fear, worry. It all came rushing in as the icy morning air chilled her to the bone.

"Have you seen him?" Rhoslyn asked, much softer.

"No, I just got here. I'm literally standing outside the hospital. I don't even know what room number he's in. My dad didn't say, and I'm not sure if he has cell service in there."

"Find a security guard, or a desk," Rhoslyn said, halting Nicolette's rambling. "They will be able to help you."

"Okay," Nicolette said, nodding as if Rhoslyn could see her.

"Everything else good?" Rhoslyn wondered. "You get there all right?"

"Sort of," Nicolette said. "Matthew Collins picked me up from the airport."

"Wait," Rhoslyn said with a little huff of laughter. "*The* Matthew Collins? The 'no man can ever compare to the sexy hockey god with the heart of gold' Matthew Collins?"

Nicolette frowned, the shiver tingling along her arms caused by much more than the Chicago cold. "Yes, well, turns out I am a terrible judge of character. He was a complete jerk. He's not like I remember at all."

"Huh, teenage girls are bad judges of character?" Rhoslyn asked dryly. "Who would've thought?"

Nicolette couldn't help but laugh, but a wooden sadness filled her as she admitted the reality. "I guess fantasies are better when they stay that way."

"Agreed. But I'm sorry anyway. It sucks that he turned out gross." Rhoslyn heaved a heavy sigh and then said, "Okay, lady. Put the shitty boy out of your head. Go find someone to help you find your brother. Go to the ER if you need to. Just start asking."

"I will," Nicolette said. "Thank you, Rhoslyn. For everything."

Just as Nicolette ended the call, a familiar car skidded to a stop, and Matthew practically flew out of the door. He thrust a cardboard caddy with four cups of coffee into her hands, then grabbed her suitcase. It made a thumping sound as he tossed it in his trunk.

"Wait here while I park," he ordered before zooming away, leaving her stunned and a little windblown on the curb.

He returned a few minutes later, jogging up to her with a grim expression.

Relieving her of the caddy, he handed her one of the cups.

"Come on," he said sternly, as if all of this was totally normal. "Austin texted me your brother's room number. I'll take you."

Without waiting for her, he marched into the hospital, and she scurried to follow.

At the elevator banks, he gestured to the cup Nicolette was clutching like a lifeline. She couldn't believe he was back. Why? Why now? The harsh hospital lights didn't dim the beauty of Matthew's face. Even at this hour, with grim severity dragging the corners of his all-too-familiar mouth down, Matthew looked luscious. His dark blue eyes zeroed in on her and Nic's chest nearly exploded with the sudden rush of heat. He watched her intently as the lift silently and swiftly carried them toward the surgical floor.

"Drink up," Matthew said, a new gentleness in his voice as he motioned toward the coffees. But no...it wasn't new. That was the gentleness that Nic remembered. That she'd wanted. She just *knew* the boy she'd loved was still in there...somewhere.

When he finally broke the stare, Nic dragged in a shaky breath. She watched Matthew as he sighed. "It's going to be a long day."

∼

THE ELEVATOR RIDE seemed to take an eternity. Matthew stood as far from Nicolette as he could, trying to school his features. He didn't want to let on what he knew. Let her hold on to normalcy for a little longer.

He had been driving for ten minutes, his brain a mushy combination of worry about making his morning appointment and worry for Nicolette. And then Austin had called.

"Where are you?" his friend demanded, his voice unnaturally harsh over the speakerphone.

"I just dropped Nicolette off," Matthew said wearily.

"Get your ass back here," Austin said, real anger creeping into his tone. "You need to bring her up to the room."

"Austin, she doesn't—"

"It's bad, Matthew," Austin said, his voice dropping to a quiet rumble. "He's in surgery."

There was a heavy pause, and Matthew realized that Austin was trying to compose himself.

"Keith is inconsolable," Austin continued, his voice scratchy. "I don't want him to have to tell Nicolette. And there's media swarming all over the place. Trying to get a fucking scoop. You need to be here, man."

There wasn't anything that Matthew wouldn't do for Austin. And this was no piddly request. His friend was hurting and needed his help.

"Okay," Matthew said finally.

"Good. See you soon." The line went dead.

There was a sign for a café on the next exit, and Matthew got off, pulling into a parking spot in front of the mom-and-pop operation. He sat with his phone cradled in his hand before typing into the search box.

He regretted doing it immediately. A long list of news coverage of the bus crash filled the screen. With shaking fingers, Matthew clicked through the first one. The picture featured something that did not resemble a bus in any form.

Metal twisted and collapsed in on itself was littered with a glittering spray of glass. The windows were warped and some of the seats lay feet from the wreckage. It was a nightmare. And Rio had been in the middle of it.

He hadn't known. He hadn't known and he'd said all those horrible things to Nicolette. He'd been so awful to her.

Tossing his phone aside, Matthew had dashed into the coffee shop, getting triple shots all around. He knew the Hayes family. He knew the drinks would be needed and welcome. He knew what he needed to do for them.

And now he was here. He could pretend Rio wasn't here—that he wasn't here for his former best friend. But Nicolette. She was innocent. She hadn't done anything and certainly didn't deserve all of the bullshit that awaited her. Matthew would protect her. If he could.

The elevator dinged, and he took Nicolette by the arm to lead her out. She looked at him in surprise but didn't pull away.

They walked out to the atrium of the surgical ward, an entire floor decorated in the generic beige of medical facilities everywhere.

Matthew pulled Nicolette into a corner, putting his body between her and the room. She wasn't a short woman, but he felt huge next to her, and the tiny space between their bodies stirred his protective instincts. He bent closer.

"Do you have a pair of sunglasses?" he asked softly.

Nicolette raised her eyebrows. "What?"

He rifled in his coat pocket and found his.

"Here," he said, pressing them into her hand. "Give me your glasses. You can see without them to walk, right?"

Nic nodded, blinking back at him in surprise. He took the stylish frames from her face. "Keep these on and stick close to me." He tucked her glasses into his coat pocket. "You can have these back in a few."

"I don't—"

"Nic." He used her nickname almost tenderly.

Nicolette listened to him with an apt expression. Her eyes were wide and without her glasses, he could see the reflection of almost every thought that raced behind them. She was looking at him with shock, worry, need. And something else.

Something that stirred Matthew in places he didn't think he'd felt before...or at least not in forever.

Matthew didn't know how this should go. Should he tuck her under his arm and ferry her to the relative safety of the room? The thought of pressing Nicolette's body to his caused an alarming uptick in his heartbeat. All those soft-looking curves and warm skin... It seemed like where she belonged. Where he wanted her. Close, tight, and where nothing could get at her sweetness.

Matthew drew in a sharp breath. This wasn't the time. The long-dormant feelings she was awakening in him had no possible outlet. He could not change ten years of anger, ten years of fortifying those walls for a pretty face. Once he dropped her off, he would get out of here. He could still make it to the inspection if he hurried. He just had to bring Nicolette through the chaos and deliver her safely. He almost rolled his eyes. Like sinking the puck and getting the hell out of the way. As if anything in his life had ever been that easy.

"There are going to be a bunch of blowhard media people here," he said, securing her glasses beside his gloves so they wouldn't get scratched. "Don't listen to anything they say and don't answer any questions."

He glanced back down at Nicolette. He carefully slid his sunglasses on her face where her own glasses once were. He tucked the stems behind her ears and smoothed her hair. He released a breath he didn't realize he was holding. Once those expressive eyes were hidden behind the mirrored lenses of his sunglasses, he could think. But now her mouth was a thin line of tension. She looked small, vulnerable, and suddenly the reality of the situation hit Matthew like a punch to the gut.

Rio was likely fighting for his life. And his little sister was in Matthew's care. Sure, he would wish himself almost anywhere but here, but it was only right to help Nicolette as much as he could, even if it was just to be a body between her and the press for the walk into the waiting room.

When Matthew fit his arm around Nicolette's shoulders, her head snapped up and her lips parted in surprise.

Being this close to her felt just as good as he'd imagined. Good and agonizing. For now, he wasn't going to overthink it. He was going to hold her tight and not let go.

"Come on," he grumbled, tugging her closer. "Just stay close."

She nodded, and together they started the long walk toward heartbreak.

The scene that appeared as they neared the surgical waiting room was exactly as Matthew had feared. Dozens of reporters milled in front of the doors, camera crews in tow. Several were scribbling notes or speaking into recording devices. Two men in suits were appealing to the hospital security guards flanking the doors.

"...five minutes," one was saying as they approached. "Come on, man, it's my job."

"It's mine too," the guard answered with an apologetic smile.

Matthew took a deep breath and steered Nicolette past the keen eyes all around them.

"We're here for Rio Hayes," he said as quietly as possible to the burly guard. But it wouldn't have mattered if he had mimed the words—a woman in sunglasses and an enormous blond man approaching the guard caused every head in the place to turn.

The security guard produced a piece of paper. "Can you write the security password here please?"

"Hey, are you a relative?" a young woman shouted, waving to a cameraman to follow her.

Matthew scribbled *Gordie Howe hat trick* on the paper, the password Austin had provided earlier.

"Who are you here for?" another reporter asked, rushing over with a tape recorder at the ready.

The guard nodded after reading the paper and opened the door a sliver to let them through. Matthew practically shoved Nicolette past the guard as the gaggle of reporters swarmed toward them. Someone bumped into him and he spun around to find a middle-aged man with a paunch trying to see over Matthew's shoulder.

"Back. *Off*," Matthew snarled, something feral rising in him at the thought of these leeches getting close enough to latch on to Nicolette.

The reporter stumbled back, and Matthew slipped through the door and slammed it shut behind him.

"You okay?" he asked, immediately reaching for the warmth of Nic. Even though he didn't need to, he tugged her back under his arm.

Her voice shook as she pulled his sunglasses from her nose. "Yeah," she mumbled, looking up at him. "Thank you."

She nestled close to him and held out her hand. Matthew stared at her palm for a moment, uncertain whether to hold it or grab her, all of her, and hold her close for just a few minutes more.

"My glasses?" she reminded him, a tiny edge of humor in her words.

"Fuck, sorry." Matthew slid her specs from his pocket. He barely touched her skin as they traded glasses, but he couldn't believe the electricity that flowed between them in that instant. A pulse in his cock reminded him that she was all grown up now. Not just his buddy's little sister, the one he'd always looked for. The one he'd seemed to need, whose constant presence had been part of everything he'd loved. This was something altogether new.

He had no time to process what he was feeling, because

almost as soon as Nic put on her glasses, she turned to face the scene in front of them and a soft, horrified gasp escaped her.

Nic stood absolutely still, her body stiff. Almost every chair in the waiting room was occupied. Faces gray with worry and streaked with tears stared back at them. An older man was pacing in the corner, worrying his thumbnail with his teeth. A pair of women in the corner were holding hands and murmuring what sounded like prayers to each other.

One woman sat with a pajama-clad child on her lap and another at her feet. She was rocking the younger child and stroking its hair.

As they surveyed the room, Nic reached out and grabbed his hand, her grip the desperate hold of someone clinging to a lifeline.

"Matthew," she whispered, still staring at the crowd gathered ahead of them.

The urge to shield her from this was fierce. Take her in his arms and get her the hell out of here. They stood there for a moment, hands clenched together, until Keith Hayes and Austin Ames crossed the room to greet them. When Nic spotted her dad, she released her hold on his fingers, and just like that, Matthew was free of his responsibility. Free of her touch. He felt the sudden emptiness and realized how familiar that hollow void was.

"Dad!" Nicolette cried.

Keith looked haggard, his graying hair sticking in every direction. Upon seeing Nicolette, he burst into tears. She wrapped her father in a hug and let him sob on her shoulder.

Austin greeted Matthew with the usual hug/back clap hybrid, then steered him a distance away, leaving Nicolette and her dad to catch up in relative privacy.

"Hey, man," Austin said softly. "Thanks for coming."

Matthew nodded, his eyes drawn back to the woman and

her children. "Do you have any details, Austin? How many injured or..."

Austin rubbed the back of his neck. "Almost the whole team was on that bus, and most of the coaching staff. Thankfully there are very few serious injuries. But a lot of worried family." Lowering his voice even further, he leaned in closer. "Rio might be the most seriously injured of all of them. Of all the fucking luck, right?"

A sticky wad of guilt slid down Matthew's throat. He'd been so dismissive before, even flippant. All that petty anger about being dragged from his bed and missing his site inspection. People's *lives* were in the balance, not to mention their hearts. Rio's life.

Of all the fucking luck.

Maybe it was more like karma. After everything Rio had done, somehow it seemed fitting to Matthew that it all might be taken away. Stripped in an unfair instant. Just like what had happened to *him*. Even as he had the thought, something in Matthew bristled. No matter how fucked up Rio was, no matter what shit he'd done to Matthew in the past, no one—no one—deserved this. This wasn't karma. This was shit. He suppressed the surge of worry and concern for his friend and focused on something less emotionally charged.

He couldn't help glancing back over at Nicolette and her dad. Keith had calmed down and was mopping his face with a tissue. Nicolette was stroking his arm and murmuring soothing words. The sight of them together, emotional father and loving daughter, was so foreign to Matthew. He doubted his parents had ever shed a tear for him, and there certainly had never been kind words or a warm touch. A fleeting thought teased him...*that could be yours. She could be.*

Before he could contemplate this, Austin nodded his head toward Nicolette.

"Come on, I think Keith and Nic are good now. I want to say hi to our girl."

They walked over and Austin opened his arms to Nicolette. She dove into his embrace like she had with Matthew, but unlike Matthew with his tense greeting, Austin held Nic for an overly long moment. Matthew ignored the dull surge of jealousy at their uninhibited hug. Austin muttered something against Nic's hair, and Nic's knuckles went white with the fierceness of her grip around his waist. When they parted, Nicolette leaned up and kissed Austin's cheek, then wiped her eyes.

"It's so good to see you, Austin," she rasped.

"You too, little sis," Austin said, squeezing her shoulder. "I've missed your baking."

"Oh!" Nicolette exclaimed, and began rummaging in her shoulder bag, a ridiculous canary-yellow thing replete with a giant bow. She produced a small bakery box and pushed it into Austin's hands.

"Here," she said, an impish half-smile bringing a light back into her eyes. "For your mama. She's supported my baking from the beginning. Did you know she sent me a gift card when I got my job so I could treat my bosses to lunch?" She paused and took a breath. "Anyway. Tell her I said hi."

Austin had a dopey smile on his face. He'd always liked Nic. Not *like*-liked. Everyone knew he'd been in love with Matthew's sister, Shelby, since forever. Everyone except Shelby, that was. Austin held the box gratefully. "Maybe you'll have a chance to tell her yourself. Can I look at them?"

A hint of red crested Nicolette's cheeks. "Of course!"

Austin lifted the top of the box and Matthew leaned in to see. Nestled in blue tissue paper were six pastel macarons. Each was a different color and they were all meticulously decorated to look like mythical creatures. A pink unicorn with a tiny gold horn. A green dragon with a toothy smile. Every detail was perfect.

They were awesome. More than that, they were impressive.

Matthew glanced at Nicolette, a little stunned. These little works of art had come from this messy, quirky, enchanting woman? Somehow it had never occurred to him that she would grow up to do something beautiful, that all those sketchbooks she'd filled would become useful to her. But here they were. Not just cookies. Not just baked goods. This was art.

Well, that explained the smell of cake, anyhow.

Suddenly a loud wail cut through the room like a siren. Everyone startled and turned to look at the little boy in the woman's lap. Fat tears were running down his face and the poor woman's efforts to shush him were proving futile.

"Hey, can I have one of those?" Matthew asked Austin, pointing to the box.

Nicolette seemed to understand what he had in mind, because the first real smile he'd seen from her blossomed on her face. "No, don't take Austin's. I have more."

Another box appeared from the depths of her purse. Matthew wondered fleetingly if there was a portal in there to a dimension filled with cookies.

Nicolette handed him the box, then patted her dad on the back. "Those were meant for you, Dad. Do you mind?"

"Of course not!" Keith said. "Go on, Matthew. I think it'll help."

Keith's eyes were starting to grow damp, and Matthew realized he'd yet to properly greet the man who had been more of a parent to him than his own. This man had been there for him when he had nothing but struggles.

And he'd repaid him by not even attending Robin Hayes's funeral.

Regret and shame filled him. No matter his problems with

Rio, he should have sucked it up and been there when Keith lost his wife. He just hadn't had the heart to face Rio...to see that asshole even if was at his mother's funeral. Matthew had known about it but didn't go. He'd spent the day in a movie theater, his phone silenced. When the credits finally rolled, he told himself Keith wouldn't have missed him. Nobody would. Nobody cared about the stowaway kid who disappeared while Rio rode his fame to the stars and back.

But now, looking at Keith across the chasm of another tragedy, it all seemed like such utter bullshit. What he held Rio responsible for...it had nothing whatsoever to do with Keith. The man who had been nothing but a near-dad to him growing up. He'd repaid the man's kindness with absence, believing that was best. Seeing the raw affection on Keith's face now, Matthew had to question himself. His actions. Too much of his past.

Unless he wanted to completely come undone, all he could do was focus on this moment.

He wasn't going to run away this time.

Handing Nicolette the box and his untouched coffee, he said, "Why don't you do it? She might feel more comfortable with you than a strange man right now."

Nicolette raised her eyebrows and accepted the box. "Sure." She looked closely at Matthew and then at her dad. As if she knew what Matthew needed, like she was reading some unwritten message in his heart, she added, "Austin, come with me?"

She tugged on Austin's sleeve and they walked over to the woman with gentle smiles.

Matthew watched for a moment, trying to buy a little bit of time before he turned to face Keith.

He was expecting censure, but Keith just smiled sadly at him. "Hi, son. Got a hug for an old man?"

As Matthew embraced Keith, a tide of emotion hit him. The walls he'd built over years and years shook like they'd been struck by a wrecking ball. Shook, but didn't fall. Matthew felt the blow deep in his chest and as he gripped the older man in a hug, he fought back the unwelcome sting of tears. Coffee or not, this was going to be a longer day than he'd anticipated.

THREE

Nicolette couldn't understand what was happening. The surgeon had just come out and informed them that Rio was doing well. But then the surgeon asked to speak to her father. Alone. She could tell the news must be bad by the way her father paled. She overheard very little. There were so many people waiting for news of loved ones, the surgical team pulled Keith aside to the most remote corner of the room they could find and they huddled close. Except Nicolette knew her father's voice. His expressions. She could vaguely make out his questions. They sounded like *Will he walk?* And *Will he ever play hockey again?*

Even though she couldn't make out what they were saying, she felt that news like this should be loud. Angry. From the sounds of it, everything her brother had worked for was gone, taken from him in a single swerve of a bus. Their lives would be forever changed. Rio's life. And his reason for living...gone. Whether he survived the crash or not, if Rio couldn't play hockey anymore...Nic had no idea who her brother would be. How he would go on. If there was ever a man who had a single focus, a single drive in life, that man was Rio. And all he'd ever wanted or loved, needed or worked toward, was hockey.

Everything became so still after the doctor delivered the news. She couldn't hear the murmuring of the others still waiting or the hum of the heating system. Just the unnatural quiet as she watched her dad walk back through the waiting room, his eyes focused on everything and nothing all at once.

"Nicolette."

Her dad squeezed her shoulder, drawing her out of the fog.

He looked awful, his eyes sunken from crying. But he was offering her a small smile, and her heart broke all over again.

"I want you to go home, kiddo," he was saying.

"No, Dad, I won't leave—" she tried, but he shook his head.

"Not up for argument. I'm still the dad and you need to sleep."

"But—I want to know..." she started.

"Babydoll," Keith said. "Let's just say the good news is your brother is alive. We're going to need to process the news over time. As a family. Tonight, all that matters is taking this step by step. He's in recovery now, and I'm going to stay with him until he's awake. Then we can trade places, okay?"

Austin stepped forward. "I'll stay with your dad, Nic. Matthew can take you home."

Nicolette couldn't think of any more arguments. If she went home, her dad would be happy. If she could provide him with even a little peace, she would. And as long as he traded places with her, a few hours' rest would probably do her good.

"Okay," she acquiesced, stepping into her dad's embrace. "But eat something, please? And try and sleep a little if you can. And make sure—"

"Nicolette," Keith gently admonished. "Go home."

Nicolette looked at Matthew and in tacit understanding, he nodded and held his arm out. She tucked under the already familiar space and lowered her face against the shouts and questions of the waiting press.

Thankfully, the reporters didn't seem interested in following them away from the surgical floor, so once they were back in the elevator, Matthew pressed the button for the lobby level and Nicolette moved out from his protective hold. She frowned a little at the loss of contact but then reminded herself it was just an arm. The warm, strong arm attached to a man she didn't even know anymore. She could miss him—who he'd been —without moving back toward him. Even though every fiber in her wanted to lean the weight and fears she was carrying against his sturdy frame. But she didn't and held her head high as she followed Matthew back through the parking lot to his car.

The car ride home was blessedly silent. Not that Matthew would have talked her ear off. Something about his familiar, quiet presence was soothing, even if he wasn't the man she'd expected him to be. Nicolette watched through the window as the sites grew more familiar the closer they got to home. The Chicago landscape was so flat compared to Colorado. Even though Nic had only been in Denver five years, she missed the panoramic view of the mountains against the early morning sky. Even still, Chicago and the gray-lit sunrise was familiar. It was home.

Finally, Matthew eased his car to a stop. The small, wood-frame Victorian where she and Rio had grown up stood like a beacon of safety against the dusky winter sky. Matthew parked the car on the street and they sat for a few moments while the years and memories collapsed between them.

"You don't have to come in," her mouth said, while her brain, against her wishes, thought, *Don't leave. Stay.*

Matthew didn't respond, though a tic in his jaw revealed some emotion. Maintaining his silence, he got out of the car and hoisted her bag from the trunk. She followed him up the walkway to the front door, where he paused, staring at the worn blue paint.

For the first time in this exhausting day, Matthew looked affected. A furrow bunched between his eyebrows and his jaw continued to tense. With a hesitant hand he reached out and touched the doorknob, resting there as if the metal offered peace.

This was his home too, Nicolette suddenly realized. Why she hadn't realized this before was beyond her. It was a consequence of having a secure and loving home, no doubt. All those questions from earlier bubbled up in her. Why he'd run away. What had happened to make him leave. How he could go from being part of everything...to nothing in what seemed like a blink of an eye. All without explanation. Not even a proper goodbye. Exhaustion and resolve combined to lower her inhibitions.

"I know that this might be rude, but I have to say this," she began, turning to face him squarely. "I'm not sure what happened between you two, but you were Rio's best friend." She shook her head. "No, it was more than that. He idolized you. Hell, *I* idolized you."

That she had not been intending to say. She bit her lip to stop her running mouth, but it was too late. Matthew's head had snapped up and he was staring at her with a mix of disbelief and awe, and something that looked like pleasure. The storm in his eyes went wild, and before she knew what was happening he was moving toward her.

He reached out and pulled her against him, engulfing her in a tight hug.

Stunned, Nicolette took a few moments to relax against him. But finally she did, welcoming the heat and the warmth and the everything that was Matthew against her. With a deep sigh, Nicolette leaned into him, winding her arms around his waist.

He felt so good. Not just the hard planes of his body or his warm hands on her back. This felt real. This felt like home, even more than the wood next to them. She held on to him like the calm in the eye of a storm and burrowed her face in his neck.

They held each other in serene silence, the only sound the cars passing by.

Nicolette could have happily stayed there for hours, surrounded by Matthew and his clean scent. But he gently pulled back, still close enough that she could see the flecks of color in his deep blue eyes.

Nicolette peered at him, trying to solve him like a puzzle. He seemed like he wanted to step away from her scrutiny, his shoulders leaning back away from her ever so slightly. Before he could leave the cocoon of their hug, she reached up and took his chin in her hand. She trailed her fingers against the stubble there, adoring the strong jaw with her curious fingertips.

"I'm going to figure you out, Matthew Collins," she said softly, unable to keep the warmth from her voice. She knew she sounded like a lovesick kid, but she didn't care. She had loved him. Maybe still did—or at least the parts of him that were still in there. Somewhere. "The past shouldn't matter anymore, don't you think?" she asked.

Matthew sighed and gently lifted his chin from her grasp.

"There's nothing to figure out," he said with a shrug. Unlike before, he didn't sound upset. Just weary and a little sad.

Nicolette finally noticed the smudges under his eyes, thrown into sharp relief by the yellow glare of the porch light. His broad shoulders were hunched as if he carried a burden too heavy even for his large frame.

An ache began to grow in the hollow of her rib cage. For all his surly attitude earlier, he'd helped her. Protected her. There was something of the Matthew she knew under there. But he wasn't fooling her now. He was hurting too...with a kind of pain that Nic wasn't sure she could understand. All she could do was guess that maybe he needed a little protecting himself.

"Do you want to come in for a bit?" Nicolette offered, patently ignoring the implications that came with that question. "You look ragged. I'm sure Dad has some wine that needs to be drunk. For its own good, of course."

Matthew paused, not reacting to her joke. Nicolette braced herself for the cold Matthew to reappear and bare his teeth. Yes, the invitation was innocent, simple. This house had been his house, and she would have invited him in no matter what. But she wouldn't lie to herself and pretend that she didn't want him there just to see if maybe the old Matthew would come back to life inside. She could hardly look at him as she waited for his answer.

"Um, yeah, actually," he finally said, checking his watch. "I'd like that. I have a few calls to make, if that's okay. Better than doing it in the car."

Nicolette nodded, trying to hide her shock mixed with delight. Best not to spook the big man. Best not to get too excited.

But Nicolette was the dictionary definition of excitable. Having Matthew coming into her house after all these years was like drinking too much coffee—she felt a jolt of delicious relief and anxiety course through her.

Her traitor hands shook as she tried to put the key in the lock, the tinkling of keys like a portent of hope after such an awful day. She stabbed the key repeatedly against the knob. Then Matthew's warm hand encircled her wrist, and he pulled the keys gently from her fingers.

He was right next to her, face bent level with hers.

He smiled at her fidgeting hands, her nervous fingers, and the smile was pure Matthew. Sweet and without guile, a whole world of possibility wrapped up in that gesture. His years seemed to melt away, but the maturity of his experiences added another layer of essential Matthew.

Heart pounding, Nicolette relinquished the keys and he opened the door, waving her in.

Nicolette flicked on lights as she went, trying to act nonchalant. It was just her house. He'd been here thousands of times. He would leave soon anyway.

Don't get excited, Nicolette warned her already beating heart.

Once she turned to face Matthew, he looked a little lost, eyes traveling the pale blue walls and oak trimmings that her parents had been so proud of.

Nothing had changed. There was the beat-up leather sofa, and the mark on the wall from when Rio and Austin had been roughhousing, Matthew looking on and laughing at his idiot friends. There was Rio's first hockey jersey, displayed in a shadow box above the stairs. Matthew must have felt like he'd stepped into a tomb, complete with artifacts preserved for all eternity.

He'd carried her suitcase in, but had stopped in the entryway, staring at a picture of her mother that hung there. It had been taken only months before she died, the symptoms of her illness evident in her face. But it was one of Nicolette's favorite pictures, her mom's humor pouring out of her saucy smile.

Matthew approached it and ran his thumb along the metal frame.

"I..." he began before lapsing into silence, his jaw tense.

"You...what?" Nicolette asked.

He caught himself, dropping his hand from the picture like

he'd been burned. His gaze was shuttered, and it seemed like jerk Matthew was back.

Nicolette wanted to push him. Did he miss her mother as much as Nicolette did? Her mom had always had a soft spot for Matthew, had always said that he could come over day or night. No invitation needed. This was his home, pure and simple. Nicolette had often wondered why Matthew would need a second home, but she never really cared as long as it meant he was there. Under their roof. His solid presence and serious grins anchoring Nic's worldview.

"Your room?" he asked suddenly, hefting the suitcase.

Nicolette nodded and followed him up the stairs.

Matthew walked with sure steps to her room at the end of the hallway. Of course he remembered exactly where to go. He pushed the door open and Nicolette heard his snort of laughter.

She peered around his shoulder. Everything was exactly the same as when she'd left it. Emerald green walls. Magenta desk scattered with old sketchbooks. Her history of science fiction poster—she really should take that home with her. The duvet cover that she'd made, covered with pictures of various fantasy and sci-fi fandoms. All the odds and ends of her young life.

"Why are you laughing?" she asked as he placed the suitcase at the foot of her bed.

Matthew shook his head. "We always thought you were so weird, Nic."

She hmphed, crossing her arms. "Weird is relative. I am *creative.*"

"I didn't mean it as a bad thing. We also thought you would make it big. We just weren't sure how." He laughed again, the sound filling her small room. "Maybe one of those artists that no one understands."

"Hey!" she cried, reaching over to give his arm a playful

pinch. He dodged out of the way and scooped up one of her sketchbooks.

"We always wondered what you were drawing," he said, beginning to flip through the colorful pages.

"Oh no! Don't—" Nicolette started, but it was too late. A pencil-and-ink drawing of Matthew in his hockey gear, mid-skate, stared back at present-day Matthew. If he were to continue turning the pages, he would find many more such renderings.

Attending hockey games had been the highlight of her teenage years. Her brother and his friends were like heroes come to life. The players made for interesting character studies, but none more than Matthew. He'd always been beautiful to her, but seeing him on the ice was next level, and she'd poured all her feelings for him onto her paper.

Mortification glued Nicolette's feet to the floor. She'd never thought she would ever feel like this again, that every flaw was on display for others to judge. That teenage shame, the not-quite-ever-fitting-in feeling. She hated that she'd ever felt it, but she'd been used to being the quirky girl at school. But not like this. Not with Matthew. As if he were immune to hearing the snickers of the popular kids or knowing how her world revolved not around her own social life but around theirs. His. Hockey and Rio and Matthew. She'd always been content to be close to them, doing what she did and what she didn't have to hide. This felt different. He'd never shown any interest in her sketchbooks, other than an arm's-length tease or good-natured joke. With one flip of the page, her entire reality shifted. He'd see her for the love-crazed stalker she was. He'd see how she'd really felt all those years. He'd see *her*.

Nic's face flamed and she took a step away from him, as if this would mitigate how crazy he must be finding her.

Matthew cleared his throat. "Um, here." He thrust the sketchbook into her arms.

She held it against her chest like armor as they stood awkwardly. She suddenly started seeing everything through Matthew's eyes. Her stuff was weird. Childish and impractical. Everything about her was slightly off, uncool. She couldn't have regretted inviting him in more than she did in this moment. At least five minutes ago, she'd still had some semblance of dignity. Her long-hidden feelings for Matthew stowed safely in the past.

"You're crazy talented, you know," Matthew said suddenly, shoving his hands deep in his pockets.

"What?" Nicolette stammered, his comment not what she had been expecting.

"I always thought so," he continued. "Your drawings were always amazing, but those cookies you made are next level."

"Thanks," she whispered.

"I remember you drawing with Shelby," he continued. "She could only manage stick figures, but she didn't care 'cause you let her keep your drawings after she finished."

Nicolette smiled at the memory. "I remember. Your parents always joked that they would sell them someday."

Nicolette immediately regretted the words. At the mention of his parents, the awkward tension from before slammed down between them. But before Matthew's face turned carefully blank, she saw deep pain in his eyes.

"I'll let you get cleaned up," he said, moving toward the door. "I gotta go make those calls." He started out the door, but paused, turning back with a gentle expression. "You really are talented, Nicolette."

Once he left, the room felt somehow smaller. Matthew had always had that presence, a gravity that did not match his quiet persona. It was one of the things she'd always liked about him.

Their lives had always been hectic, and Matthew had been the lodestone that held them in place.

She hadn't realized how much she'd craved that until now.

Digging in her suitcase, she grabbed a nearly threadbare T-shirt she'd been gifted during welcome week at culinary school and some PJ pants with multi-colored macaroons with wings. A quick shower made her feel like a new person. She brushed her teeth and returned to her room, shoving her dirty clothes in the corner.

Brushing out her hair, Nicolette glanced at the sketchbook lying on her bed, like a physical piece of the past. It was so surreal that he was here again, talking about Rio and Austin. She had noticed he'd always referred to them as "we." They'd been a unit, a team, closer than friends. They'd all been a part of something bigger.

More than that, they'd been a family. Nicolette still didn't know what had happened to change that, but she knew those memories were real and vital. They were for her as well. Maybe more real than the present.

She looked at the wall above her desk. She'd strung lights and hung pictures from painted clothespins. She and her parents at a Cubs game. Her hugging Rio after his team won the local championships. Austin, Matthew, and Rio holding her like a mermaid on her fourteenth birthday.

These boys—men now—had shaped who Nicolette was. Even though she'd often tried to hide her talent, they'd always shown her the right way to live.

And then Matthew left them. And Mom died.

Her family and her art had saved her, from bullies and just generally marching to her own drum. And now Matthew was here again, and he was nothing like she remembered. Worse, it seemed like he'd forgotten what it had all meant. She'd seen glimpses of the real Matthew. But he seemed buried under distance and pain that she didn't understand.

Nicolette sighed and put the sketchbook back on the desk. She wanted to revel in the good memories. She knew there was no going back. And with the question marks about Rio's recovery and her job, the future was uncertain at best.

But that smile on Matthew's face convinced her of one thing—she would do everything she could to help her family heal. Her father, her brother, Matthew.

Things could never be the same.

But maybe they could be better.

MATTHEW PACED THE LIVING ROOM, waiting for Chris Kinsman to answer his phone. Chris was his contractor and usually answered on the first ring. But five rings in and there was no answer, and Matthew was grinding his jaw.

"Matthew!" Chris's jovial tone finally came through the receiver. "What's up? We're still on for today, right?"

"I can't make it," Matthew grumbled. "I was up all night. My...friend was on the bus that crashed yesterday."

"Oh man, yeah, I saw that," Chris said with true sympathy. "Is there anything I can do? Anything you need?"

"No," Matthew said, softening his tone. "I just need to reschedule, but I'm not sure for when."

"Of course, anytime."

"Sorry about all this," Matthew said, feeling pulled in too many directions.

"Don't apologize." It was Chris's turn to sound gruff. "Family always comes first, okay?"

This brought Matthew up short, his feet pausing again before the picture of Robin Hayes.

Though his parents were still very much alive, they were about as reachable as poor Robin was.

An image of the bus crash flashed through his mind. What if something like that were to happen to one of his siblings? God knew Jackson was a walking disaster, always jetting halfway across the world on some harebrained scheme. Would anyone even know whom to call if something happened to his brother a million miles from home? His parents never kept the same phone long enough for him to recognize their number. He might miss an important call about them and never even know before it was too late.

Matthew finally answered Chris after too long a beat. "Yeah, family first. Thanks, man."

"And take care of yourself too," Chris continued. "I know what you're like, Matthew."

"Charming and irresistible?" Matthew asked, not wanting Chris to worry.

The other man laughed. "Not what I was thinking, but sure, buddy. Just keep me updated."

Matthew ended the call just as Nicolette reached the landing. His blood warmed as she walked toward him. Hair damp from a shower, she wore a loose shirt and patterned PJ pants. Her feet were bare and she pushed her glasses up on her nose as she approached.

In this completely unassuming getup, she oozed an ease and comfort that Matthew was drawn to. He tracked a smattering of freckles across her cheeks, and the tiny mole just under her bottom lip. Her full hips were perfectly visible under the thin fabric of her pants and—Jesus Christ, he could see her nipples poking through her shirt.

What was it about this girl? A pair of doe eyes and some cute PJs and, shit... Matthew felt like a teenage boy again.

Apparently blithely unaware of Matthew's blood suddenly

surging south, Nicolette walked past him into the kitchen and started rifling through a cupboard, giving him an unobstructed view of her plush ass.

"Wine?" she called over her shoulder.

"Oh, god, yes," he said, his dry throat practically screaming for lubrication, along with other parts of his body.

She threw him a puzzled look over her shoulder, but commenced her search, moving to the next cupboard.

Unable to resist the show, Matthew leaned against the bar and watched as Nicolette rummaged through the kitchen. He couldn't help but chuckle.

"What?" she asked.

"Nothing. Just never imagined I'd see innocent little Nicolette raiding the cupboards for booze."

"Hey!" she said, turning around, crossing her arms under her breasts. "I'll have you know I took part in my fair share of underage drinking, thank you very much."

Keeping his eyes determinedly on her face, he gave her a skeptical look. "Uh-huh. Did you and your friends share two light beers between you at a sleepover once?"

Nicolette stuck her nose in the air. "Please. For your information, it was a bottle of hard lemonade, and I even felt tipsy."

Matthew laughed, a true laugh, and he felt some of the tension in his neck release. He hadn't laughed like that in ages.

Nicolette was beaming at him, her grin wide. He didn't want this to stop. This banter, this connection. It was familiar and yet not old, not overdone. The crackle of humor between them was as welcome as touching her in the hospital had been —like this was something he should never have lost. Correction —never have let go. But he couldn't let himself think about teenage Nic when the very womanly version of her was bending over and revealing of slip of skin between her waistband and her shirt.

"Well, miss party pants," he said, nearly choking on a chuckle as he very closely kept an eye on her *pants*, "where's the wine then?"

"I know he has some," she muttered, returning to the search. "Anyway, it's not like *you* guys drank. Straight as arrows I'm sure."

"There may have been a few indiscretions," he drawled, delighting in her laugh as she checked the pantry.

"Indiscretions my ass," she said. "I bet what my parents didn't know saved them many a gray hair."

"It's true," he admitted. "The stories I could tell you... You can't even imagine the shenanigans. Some of the shit that happened after hockey games..." The word, for the first time in years, didn't catch in his throat. *Hockey.* He'd said it and he didn't even feel like smashing a fist through a wall. Rio Hayes's wall no less.

Although if Matthew were being honest, he probably could have recited Rio's stats from memory while watching Nicolette's fine ass waving around and done it with a smile. What was it about this girl—this woman—that made even the pain of the past seem a little less painful?

"Voila!" she crowed. She stood up, clutching four bottles of wine by their necks. "Behind the dish soap, of course. Because Dad is weird like that."

"I see where you get your weird," Matthew teased, taking the bottles from her.

"That was low-hanging fruit," she scolded, now searching for glasses.

Matthew read the labels on the wine. The fatigue was starting to catch up with him, and he wondered if wine was a good choice.

"Maybe we should have coffee?" he suggested as Nicolette

reappeared with two wine glasses. "I have to head home at some point."

"Stay here," Nicolette said with a little shrug, as if this was no big deal. "You can crash in Rio's room."

He was about to tell her absolutely not but she continued. "I've never actually stayed in this house by myself. I'd really love the company."

Her tone was light, but there was a vulnerability there that Matthew couldn't ignore.

"All right," he said, and her smile was all the reward he needed.

"Yay! You can always call your girlfriend and let her know you'll be spending the night with a beautiful woman."

"A beautiful woman with wine," he responded, and then realized what he'd said. That he found her beautiful. It wasn't a lie, so he let the words linger. It was true. She deserved that. A little compliment to counteract the teasing. She wouldn't read anything more into it than that.

"Come on," she said, gesturing to the living room, where that old sofa beckoned.

Matthew sank down beside her, blessing Keith for being as typical a dad as he could have wished for. The sofa had to be at least ten years past its expiration date, and yet here it was...the same one he'd stretched his legs on a kid. He made a futile attempt at fluffing a throw pillow that was practically flattened into the shape of Keith's head while Nic popped the cork from the first bottle. She poured them both generous portions and raised her brows at the nearly flat pillow.

"I know what Dad's getting for Christmas this year," she teased.

"You can't replace the couch," he said, giving up on the throw pillows and leaning back against the cushions. "After all this time, it's practically a member of the family."

"I can't afford to replace the couch!" she said, swatting him lightly on the arm. "But I think a couple of pillows fit into a baker's budget."

"A cookie artist," he corrected.

She looked at him, her face reflecting her surprise at his praise. "Thank you," she said softly, the vibe between them noticeably changed at his words, at his acknowledgment of her.

There was something so good about this. A quiet house. A comfortable seat. A glass of wine with someone he knew—and cared about deeply. And he did care for Nic. Always had.

He hadn't realized it, but sitting next to Nic, the curve of her thigh in those crazy-ass pajama pants so close to his...he could see now that he had been lonely. And on some level he'd never really allowed himself to want more. Wanting meant being open to the disappointment of not getting. And he'd had enough disappointment and not getting in this lifetime.

He glanced at Nicolette. Her wine-stained lips were soft as she contemplated him.

"What?" he asked, genuinely curious about what she saw.

"Why aren't you married?" she asked, and he almost laughed at her astuteness.

"I have to fight them off," he said, nudging her foot with his. "Couldn't disappoint the legion of ladies beating a path to my door by settling down with just one." The contact sent a buzz of sensation up his foot directly to his crotch. He wasn't sure where this humorous mood was coming from. Probably the wine. He took another sip. He'd lost track of the number of glasses they'd shared... Nic seemed as intent on refilling them as he seemed on emptying them.

"You sound like Rio," she said with a grimace. "He thinks that women would, like, kill themselves if he settled down."

Matthew shook his head. "He was always like that." Not

wanting to talk about Rio, Matthew turned her question back on her. "What about you? Is there a boyfriend in Denver?"

Please say no, he thought.

"Nah, never had the time, and no one was ever interested. Apparently I'm a little intimidating."

Matthew nearly choked on his wine. "What kind of men are you hanging around with?"

"Dumb ones," she said with a surly glance into her wineglass. "They like to eat the cookies but not take home the baker." She paused, blinking owlishly for a moment. "God, that sounded dirty."

Matthew placed a placating hand on her knee and squeezed. "You get a pass. I think we've demolished two bottles."

Nicolette surveyed the table. "Shit, you're right. Well, we deserve it, all things considered."

They sat in silence for the next few moments. Her knee was warm under his palm, her thigh temptingly close. The alcohol was humming pleasantly in his veins and, even freshly showered, Nicolette smelled like a goddamn dessert. He breathed in deeply, his eyes fluttering shut.

"I guess it's bedtime," she was saying.

Matthew's eyes flew open. He didn't want to get up. He was more relaxed than he could remember being in years. And worse—or better—he was having fun. He was happy. Nicolette was starting to get under his skin. He knew her. And yet she was completely new.

And shit, he was drunk.

They rose from the couch, and Matthew caught Nicolette's arm when she swayed.

"Thanks," she said, smiling sweetly up at him. "Coming upstairs?"

Lust jolted Matthew into sobriety. An invitation upstairs

was an invitation to that beguiling body. He could strip away the thin cotton and see for himself how luscious he suspected she was. Her hot skin under his hands, her lips against his...

His cock was rapidly hardening when she yawned and said, "There's still some of Rio's clothes up there, you can come pick some out."

Right. Of course. Damn wine was making him horny. He needed to remember whom he was with and why he was here.

He was wearing a T-shirt under his button-down and he could sleep in his boxer briefs. There was really no need to go upstairs at all. He'd never actually sleep in Rio's clothes—the idea nearly made him gag. This wasn't a schoolgirl's sleepover. But somehow the idea that he would had Nicolette already halfway up the stairs and motioning for him to follow her.

And how he wanted to follow. Not because he thought he might get lucky. He hoped he wasn't that big of a creep. But because he wanted to be near her as long as possible.

Nicolette turned on the landing and waited for him, the hall light casting long shadows. She didn't move farther up the stairs as he reached the landing. She just waited for him until he stood inches away, towering over her. She might not have been short, but next to him she looked delicate as she craned her neck to meet his gaze.

A wicked smile passed over her lips. "I used to sit here and eavesdrop on your conversations, you know. You guys were so loud I could hear everything. Learned a lot about sex that way."

"Ew," Matthew said with a smile. "And I'm sorry. You probably didn't exactly learn much."

"That's true," Nicolette laughed. "But it was like gossip. I couldn't get enough. And you were always so quiet. I would always wait for you to say something."

She bit her lip and looked away, and the sudden realization hit Matthew like a truck. She'd always waited for him to talk?

She'd said before she'd admired him, but maybe it had been more. His thoughts raced to the sketches... He suddenly wished he'd flipped through the entire book, all of her books. Just to see whom she'd drawn, carefully, lovingly, page after page, year after year.

He looked into her flushed face, her eyes still turned away, and he realized something he should have always known. They were all of him. It had always been him. Nic orbiting not just Rio, not just the Terrible Trio because they were part of her brother's universe. Nic had always been attached to one guy's words, one guy's face, one guy's every move. His.

It was something he'd always known, hadn't he? Something he'd taken for granted. Her watchful, close presence wasn't just that of a little sister with nothing better to do than shadow her big brother and his boisterous friends.

Maybe he'd always wanted her attention to mean more. Because he sure as fuck wanted it to mean more now.

There were no alarm bells ringing as he swayed toward her, just an overwhelming feeling of rightness. But still he paused, her alcohol-tinted breath cresting over his sensitized lips. This wasn't the right time, no matter the desire he thought he read on her face, matching his own. He waited for any sign of hesitation from her, anything that she might do to correct his confused thinking, set him straight about her feelings. He waited for absolutely any sign that he was dead-bang deluded, completely and totally wrong.

His uncertainty was short lived. Before Matthew could think or hope, Nicolette took his face in gentle hands and pulled him to her. She pressed a soft, sweet kiss on his mouth. It was practically over before it began, just a touch. Not nearly enough. Nicolette didn't pull away after, a challenge in her green eyes and a gentle huff that promised passion sighing against his face.

The wanting crashed through any of Matthew's good judgment. Just this once, he didn't want to be the sensible one. He wasn't going to be the solid older-brother type protecting her from danger. He was the danger. Grabbing Nicolette by the hips, he pulled her roughly against his body, and kissed her back.

This was no chaste kiss between friends. Their mouths crashed together, and he moved over hers in long, thorough movements. He coaxed her open with his tongue, and with a guttural moan he slipped his tongue inside. The heat of her mouth melted him like butter. Nicolette fisted her hands in the front of his shirt, pulling him closer, and the feel of her against him was better than he could have imagined. Needing more, he moved his hands on a scorching path from her hips down to her ass. He'd wanted this since she came down those stairs in those ridiculous pants...maybe since he'd spotted her diving for her suitcase at baggage claim. Maybe for even longer than that.

He held her ass in his hands and drew her closer, her supple body melding against him like it belonged there. Like it fit. And it did. As they traded needy, exploring kisses, Nic worked her fingers through Matthew's hair at the back of his head. Every inch of his skin came alive under her touch, and when she leaned back just far enough for Matthew to snake a hand beneath her T-shirt, he couldn't resist more, feeling more, taking more. Her fragrance was stronger this close and he quickly got lost in a plume of vanilla-scented desire. Feeling his way through, he slid a hand higher, past the curve of her ribs until his fingertips glanced the globe of her breast.

And then she gasped, a small, breathy sound. It wasn't a negative sound—not the sign to stop or a clue that she was feeling any sort of hesitation. It was quite the fucking opposite. Nic drew in a breath so ragged, so aroused at his touch that reality suddenly hit Matthew like a punch to the gut. He was kissing Nicolette Hayes. And they were well on their way to something more.

This couldn't happen. He couldn't throw away his sanity for this woman, no matter how beguiling she was. It would never work.

He tried to be gentle when he pushed her away, but even through her desire-blown eyes he could see a shimmer of hurt.

Unable to explain, he just shook his head and offered her a sad smile. "How about that T-shirt?"

Something like pride filled him at how quickly she composed herself. She was strong. She'd be okay.

"Um, yeah," she said, tugging her shirt straight. "They're in Rio's room."

Matthew could have found Rio's room blindfolded, but he let her lead the way. And proceeded to be a coward, hovering on the threshold. He could see Rio's hockey trophies lined up on his dresser. Rio's collection of classic novels sat untouched on his desk. "I like having secret depths," Rio had always joked when they'd teased him about it. Even his prized signed Gretzky stick was propped in the corner just where it always had been.

Nicolette pulled a shirt and pajama pants from Rio's dresser, and dumped them in his arms.

"The sheets are clean," she said, gesturing to the bed. Her tone was cool and polite.

"No," Matthew said too quickly. "I mean, I'll just crash on the couch."

There was no way he was sleeping in Rio's room. Thankfully, though she raised an eyebrow, she didn't argue with his decision.

"Wait here," she said, and ducked down the hallway, reappearing a few seconds later with a pillow and a brightly colored afghan. He recognized the blanket as one of Robin's and wondered what he'd done to deserve this.

They stood awkwardly in the hallway, the bedding in his arms a barrier between them.

"Well, good night," he said, cringing at his awkwardness.

He turned to go down the stairs but paused when she said his name.

"Matthew."

He looked back over his shoulder, his heart stopping at how beautiful she was. Her lips were still swollen from his kiss, her eyes ablaze with the traces of the shared passion he still felt surging through his body.

"Yeah?" he managed.

"Don't leave." Her words were soft and cut him to the fucking core. Her tired eyes sparkled with something sad, something that let him know she was opening herself to him. Don't run away, she meant. Don't sneak out when no one's looking. What he imagined was that she was asking him not to run *again*. "Okay?" she asked, smoothing her kiss-mussed hair.

He almost laughed. She really understood him. Nic *knew* him. Even after all this time, she could see through the façade to the man. He'd planned on doing just that.

But he'd done enough damage here today. He could do this one thing for her.

"I won't," he promised, before turning and leaving her standing at the top of the stairs.

FOUR

Snuggled in a pile of pillows, Nicolette tried to relax. Her family always loved to tease her about her penchant for sleeping in what was basically a pillow fort. She'd never been able to fully explain how cozy it made her feel. Like she was wrapped in clouds.

Now the clouds had turned stormy, and it was all thanks to the ridiculously attractive man currently stretched out on the couch downstairs.

She'd kissed him. *She'd kissed him.* She now knew what Matthew Collins tasted like, what his body felt like beneath his clothes. She knew how he kissed and how he touched, and the answer to all of this was that he was unbearably sexy. Better than her girlish fantasies, because Matthew had grown into quite the man.

All that potential was sleeping just a floor away, and her brain would not be contained. She couldn't count how many times she'd dreamed of Matthew, even into adulthood. Her dreams had always been slightly innocent, a kiss here or a touch there. Even as a teenager, Nicolette had a weird superstition that imagining sex with Matthew would jinx her, that if she did, it would never happen.

But now that she'd had a taste of his wine-soaked lips, her body pulsed with an urgency at his presence and her thoughts took a turn into downright dirty territory.

How easy would it be to slip downstairs and tell him she wanted him? He might be hesitant, but his desire would overwhelm his qualms. She'd shed her clothes while he watched, then help him pull his own off. She'd climb onto his lap, and he'd kiss down her neck, lips hot on her needy skin. She'd trail her hand down his hard body, and feel his thick cock stiffen against her...

Nicolette sat upright in the bed. This was *so* not helping.

Groaning, she put her head in her hands. Her brother might never play hockey again and she was dreaming about fucking his best friend. Former best friend. Whatever. Added to that was the fact that her own future was up in the air... She didn't have time to be a giggly teenager with the same old hopeless crush. Or was it hopeless? Matthew's kiss hadn't exactly been something he was forced to do. Nic's nipples hardened as she replayed the feeling of his fingers on her skin over and over in her mind.

A pang to talk to her mother hit Nicolette so hard it hurt. Mom would have known what to do, what to say. She would have listened to Nicolette's problems and taken care of Dad. She would have known how to support Rio, and she would have made sure nothing fell through the cracks. Blue Hippo, work... Mom would even have known exactly what to do about Matthew.

"That boy," she remembered her mother saying. "One day he'll wake up and realize what a gem he is. The world had better watch out when he does, not to mention the women."

She'd thrown a knowing look at Nicolette. "Though some people already know, don't they?"

Nicolette had never breathed a word about her crush to anyone, but Mom knew. She went out of her way to understand people and knew how to make everyone feel special. Mom made friends wherever she went and was always the first one to offer a friendly ear or a shoulder to cry on.

Memories flooded her in a wave, but Nicolette let them come. They made her feel close to her mom, and that was worth the pain that inevitably came too. The tears were just evidence of the depth of her love.

The Thanksgiving Nicolette was thirteen came to the front of her mind. She'd always loved Thanksgiving—though at eleven she had become politicized and always made sure to mention the injustice the holiday represented. Rio of course teased her mercilessly, but Nicolette would not be swayed.

But the holiday was special because Austin and Matthew would always spend the night. Austin's mom ran a diner and chose to cater to those who needed a hot meal when everyone else was closed. And Matthew...well, his parents just never seemed like they were around.

They had their traditions, the kind that all families had. No one was really sure how they had started, but they stuck to them religiously all the same. Breakfast was blueberry pancakes and hot chocolate. Hopped up on sugar, the boys would head out back to pass a puck around until the football game came on, sometimes joined by the next-door kids.

Nicolette was always stuck between helping her dad prepare the feast and watching the boys. Usually she'd attempt to help Dad until he shooed her out. Then she'd sit in a deck chair pretending to sketch while sneaking glances at Matthew. His smile was a rare thing, but when they goofed around like that he couldn't seem to stop. Nicolette always felt a funny ache in her chest watching him, a feeling too big for a kid to understand.

Mom would call them in and ply them with snacks for the game and then settle in to watch with them. She usually cheered louder than anyone, for both teams, earning embarrassed admonishments from Rio.

Dad would announce dinner, his meticulously crafted feast crowned by a turkey far too large for the six of them. He didn't care, saying the turkey soup and sandwiches were worth it. Everyone would happily stuff themselves and the boys would retreat to the basement for a marathon of video games and even more food.

"Where do they put it all?" her mom asked that Thanksgiving, with a mix of awe and disgust as she prepared bowls of chips and dip. "Maybe I should take up hockey."

Nicolette giggled as she sketched cookie ideas. She'd just started baking and was bursting to the seams with ideas of how her art could fit on a baked surface.

"Mom, you'd be terrible at hockey," Nicolette reasoned, watching as her mom put some carrots and broccoli alongside the ranch dip. As if the boys would touch them. But that was Mom.

Nicolette's mom gave her a strangely disapproving look. "You don't know that." She paused, considering her daughter. "Listen, kiddo. I know you're pretty okay with being you. But sometimes we need others to support us, even if we are doing something stupid."

"Okay, what?" Nicolette said. Mom was having a "serious" moment, and it was always good to listen.

"Don't give up because of circumstances, Nicolette," her mom said softly. "And don't be afraid to ask for help." Her mom glanced toward the basement door. "It's something Matthew could stand to learn."

"Matthew's perfect," Nicolette had blurted, a furious blush rising to her cheeks.

Mom's tinkling laugh dispelled the heavy mood. "Oh, honey. You've got it bad."

Not much changed in the ensuing years. The boys were thick as thieves and Nicolette basked in their secondhand glow. They seemed destined for the same future, a life of hockey fame and fortune, brothers on the ice and off.

Until Matthew disappeared, and Nicolette would recall her mother's words. If Matthew had needed help, he would have asked them. Right? But everyone seemed to forget that Matthew even existed and went on as before. Nicolette wondered, as impossible as it seemed, if maybe Matthew had done something wrong. There didn't seem to be any other reason why Rio would never again talk about his best friend.

Things got busier and Nicolette had less time to wonder what had happened to the boy she'd dreamed about. While Rio's hockey career took off, Nicolette had a full schedule of art and pastry classes. Her style had caught the attention of some bloggers and she put together an impressive portfolio. She just needed professional experience.

Nicolette and Rio left home at the same time, Rio to Italy for a hockey development program and Nic to Denver. She'd been accepted to a Baking and Pastry Arts program and had managed to snag a part-time job that would later lead to full-time work with Luz.

Busy balancing school and work, Nicolette usually fell into bed exhausted at the end of the day. In her quiet moments, homesickness dogged her. Memories of everything she'd left behind seemed more real than the future she could envision.

She'd been considering a trip home when she'd gotten the call. Her mom was dying and she needed to come immediately if she wanted to say goodbye.

To this day, the anger and agony that surrounded her mom's death made Nicolette want to scream to the sky at the unfairness of it. Her mom had told her to ask for help and yet didn't do it for herself until it was too late.

The doctors told them later that her mom had had an ulcer that she had not sought treatment for. The ulcer had ruptured and her darling, stubborn mother, despite debilitating pain, had waited for her husband to come home from work instead of calling him at the first signs of distress. She could barely stand by the time Keith got home. Two days later, sepsis had set in and there was nothing to be done.

Nicolette hadn't made it in time. They took her mom off life support a few minutes after Nicolette arrived. But she was already gone by that time. There would be no hugs, no sweet parting words. Nic waited at her mom's bedside for as long as they would let her. Robin's skin was still warm, and she looked so *Mom*. Even after she knew that she was gone. Nicolette lost it, sinking to her knees beside the bed and sobbing until finally her father gently pried her away.

He seemed lost, alternating between desperate tears and a strange blankness that scared Nicolette, so that her despair quickly shifted to anger. Anger was easier to feel.

They'd somehow made it home after arranging the final details before Nicolette rounded on her father.

"How could she do this?" Nicolette had railed. "How could you not know?"

"I guess she didn't want to burden us," her dad said softly. Despite her anger, he had yet to let go of her hand, and he gave it a gentle squeeze. "She always put us first."

"But the doctor said she must have been in pain for months!" Nicolette cried, wanting to tear her hair out. "How could she be so idiotic?"

"Nicolette!" her father scolded. "Don't talk about your mother that way!"

But Nicolette was too far gone. She ripped from her father's grasp and began pacing the living room.

"One doctor's visit and she would still be here. She chose to leave us!"

"Nic, calm down," her dad said, sounding a little worried.

"And where the fuck is Rio?" she spat, pointing to the door as if her brother was about to swoop through, bringing that whiff of ice that followed him. "Is hockey so important he couldn't be at his own mother's deathbed?"

"He called, he said—"

"I don't care what he said!" she roared. "What is wrong with this family? I—"

Suddenly her eyes caught on a picture on the mantle. It had been taken at Nicolette's sixth birthday. Her mom had thrown her a unicorn-themed party, painstakingly planning every last detail. The picture showed Nicolette in the dress her mom had made, patterned with tiny unicorns and bordered with rainbow ribbons. Nicolette was hamming it up for the camera, but Robin's eyes were on her daughter. Her expression was one of pure love.

And now that woman was gone.

Nicolette made it to the bathroom in time for her lunch to make a violent reappearance.

"Nicolette?" her dad had said tentatively from the doorway.

"Just give me a minute, please?" Nic gasped, and guilty relief filled her at her dad's retreating footsteps.

She flushed the toilet and plopped down beside it. Somehow, she felt a little better, like she'd purged poison from her body.

"Throwing up is the best," Matthew had said to her once

when she'd gotten food poisoning and was feeling sorry for herself. "It sucks when you're doing it, but you're getting all the bad stuff out."

God, how she'd wished Matthew was there when her mom died. She'd craved his steady presence and gentle smile. He would have known how to handle her dad and Rio. He'd have been quiet but understanding—angry along with her even if he didn't show it quite as dramatically as she had.

He would have known what to do. Somehow he would have helped her ease into her new reality—one where things didn't always work out, and parents were vulnerable. No matter how much she planned her life, she had no control. But even that was a child's fantasy. Weeks, months passed. No one saw or heard a peep from Matthew Collins.

He wasn't there, hadn't been for years. Another fallible hero.

Rio never came home either.

There never was a funeral. As far as she knew, Mom's ashes were still sitting in a box in the back of Dad's closet. He had never really come to terms with her loss. He'd withdrawn, just worked and puttered around an empty house. And Rio barely visited, maybe stopping in on his way to somewhere else. In many ways, their family broke the day her mom died. The first fracture had been losing Matthew. The rest of her happy life disappeared with her mom.

"Shit," Nicolette muttered, crashing back to reality to find her face wet with tears. This was why she didn't drink. Getting wasted only led to horny thoughts and depressing memories. She'd checked both boxes and was now wasted *and* miserable.

She could scarcely believe this was happening to her again. As if losing her mother too soon wasn't enough, now Rio was broken. She could only hope her father wouldn't break too.

But at least Rio would survive. No matter the pain he was

in, he would continue to breathe. And Nicolette could work with that.

A new resolve stiffened Nicolette's spine—she wasn't going to make the same mistakes this time. She wouldn't let everyone fall apart alone. She would fight with every last breath to bring them all together, to keep them safe. Rio and her dad needed her on the long road to recovery. She would channel her mother's spirit and put them first. Maybe she could put her family back together in the process. And that family included Matthew Collins.

And she couldn't deny that Matthew's reappearance in her life was exciting and terrifying. The kiss had affected her more than she wanted to admit, but she wasn't going to let him escape so easily, no matter where that went. She would get to the bottom of whatever his hangup was and pull him back into the fold. And if it meant more hot kisses, all the better.

Tomorrow. Tomorrow she would see Rio in person and see for herself what she had to do to help him. She would confront Matthew and make everything okay. And once everything was tied in a neat little bow, she could get back to Denver and see about applying for the comic con. Easy, and not emotionally draining at all.

Nestling back into her cocoon, Nicolette fell into a fitful sleep, chased by the scent of her mother's perfume.

MATTHEW STOOD in the middle of the living room in a daze, Rio's clothes in his hands and Nicolette's taste on his lips. Why had he thought it was a good idea to put his mouth, or any body part for that matter, on Nicolette Hayes? Now everything was muddled. A clean break from this situation was no longer possible, and Matthew wasn't entirely sure he minded.

Shit. Wine wasn't enough. Glancing around the room, he remembered that Keith kept a bottle of scotch behind the encyclopedias, thinking the boys would never want to look there. He'd apparently forgotten the tenacity of teenage boys on a quest to get hammered.

Of course, Keith had probably stopped hiding his liquor long ago. But Matthew slid the heavy volumes aside and laughed. There was an unopened bottle of decent scotch, the memory of them taking tiny sips to hide the evidence making him smile. Some things never changed. Even the glass he pulled from the cupboard was familiar, one of Robin's National Park tumblers. It was a small comfort.

Matthew couldn't bring himself to put on Rio's old clothes, despite feeling a bit grimy. He shucked his shoes, button-down, and jeans, and poured himself a measure of scotch, just enough to ease his churning thoughts. Collapsing onto the couch, he heaved a weary sigh. The worn leather cradled his body like a hug, and for one blissful moment everything was quiet.

And then the words Nicolette had spoken on the porch came roaring back at him.

"I'm going to figure you out, Matthew Collins. The past shouldn't matter anymore, don't you think?"

All the reasons why he'd stayed away from this family slammed into him. He'd been lulled into a sense of ease by the familiar, Keith's kindness at the hospital, and the warm memories in this house. Austin calling in favors. Returning to this place where he had once belonged.

And Nicolette in his arms, her lush mouth open under his, that sweet smell of hers igniting him. She'd completely given over to him, her small sounds of passion showing him what he dreamed of in the darkest part of the night. Want. Need. Affection.

The way she looked at him, as if he was strong and good.

She'd said she idolized him.

Matthew could count on one hand the serious relationships he'd been in. Not one of those women had looked at him the way Nicolette did.

He'd worked so hard to be that man, the one who was enough. To separate himself from the corruption that had destroyed his family and his life. Though he was what anyone would call a success, there wasn't a day when he thought that he was good enough. Why else had those who were supposed to love him treated him like nothing?

And yet here Nicolette was, acting like he was something special, that he had mattered to her then and still did even now. Without Rio. Without hockey.

He leaned back against the pillow and her sweet scent floated around him, making his mouth water. Who could have guessed that Nicolette would grow up with the ability to press every one of his buttons? She had just been a slightly pesky kid to him, a member of a singular family that he'd once been a part of. They'd both been kids, really. And now here they were. It seemed like he wasn't meant to escape her.

It was strange how tied up his past really was with Nicolette and her family. Even the fact that Nicolette had ended up in Denver seemed like a strange twist of fate, their paths entwined in some unknowable way. That she would choose the place he himself had chosen made his head spin. Denver had been his dream, and it ended up supporting hers.

Had she realized it when she chose? Did she vaguely remember that he'd been set to move there for school? His decision, after all, had not been very popular in the Hayes household.

Matthew, for all his love of hockey, was never quite as good as Rio and Austin. They were the golden twins who pulled him along in their wake. People rarely noticed Matthew without

Rio first pointing him out. Matthew never minded. He wasn't much for the spotlight and he had accepted the truth a long time ago. Rio was the star. He was happy to support his friend any way he could.

College had always been Matthew's goal, out of both desire and necessity. With a good hockey scholarship, he could still play while ensuring a future away from his parents. The University of Denver had a great team, and many players were drafted after a few years of playing. It gave him options, something he'd never really had before. And DU was offering him a full ride, which meant freedom. Anything to get away from his parents.

Rio was not impressed.

"You're throwing your talent away!" he'd argue whenever the topic came up.

This was easy for Rio to say. He'd been garnering attention all through high school and was being courted by a development program based in Italy. Almost all the participants went on to play professional hockey. Rio's spot was guaranteed, and he wanted Austin and Matthew with him, the Terrible Trio on the road.

"Shit, Matthew, think of all the girls!" Rio said in true Rio form. "Not to mention the money. Why don't you want to go pro?"

"He still can," Austin pointed out, by this time weary of hearing this argument. "Plenty of college players do."

"But why wait?" Rio insisted. "You're just gonna get fat and slow. Or injured."

How could he explain to Rio that he needed a fallback, that he couldn't rely on his family to support him if things went south? There were so many ways for a professional athlete's career to end suddenly. Matthew needed the security of a college degree, and hopefully pro-level hockey would be a possibility.

But Rio never really understood this, and badgered Matthew even up to graduation day.

"There's still time," he said as they stood waiting to receive their diplomas. "I could put in a good word with my agent."

Matthew knew Rio meant well. But getting by on Rio's left-overs was unacceptable. He might not be the most confident person, but he still had his pride.

As it turned out, pride was not worth very much.

A week before Matthew was meant to move to Denver, his parents got into some legal trouble. At first it seemed like just a lot of smoke and noise, but they'd been arrested. Matthew had been at practice when his parents were taken away. Shelby had been under Nic's watchful care in the corner of the rink. Only Jackson had been home, alone, when two plainclothes detectives from Chicago PD came and took their parents away. Since Jackson had been sixteen at the time, the cops left him home alone. When he broke the news to Matthew, Jackson had cried. It was the first and last time Matthew remembered seeing his brother moved to tears.

His parents made a deal with the prosecutor and pled out to fines and a string of lesser offenses, but the damage was already done. Matthew received a terse email informing him that not only was his scholarship revoked, but he was no longer welcome at DU. Somehow DU had gotten wind of his parents' fraud arrest. They looked into his scholarship application and found "irregularities." They rescinded the offer of funding and his spot on the team. Which meant college, for Matthew, was officially over before it began. Just like his hockey career. And his life.

He didn't know which was worse—what his parents had done, or the fact that he was actually surprised. He'd always known they were involved in things that bordered on questionable. He knew they were selfish and unconcerned with the rules. It was why he spent so much time with his hockey family—his parents never seemed that interested in parenting.

And yet he was still devastated that they would knowingly drag him down with them. That they would so carelessly take away his chance at happiness. His naiveté made their actions even harder to take, because now he was disappointed in himself.

After reading the letter from DU, he'd headed straight to Rio's house in a stupor. He was empty with shock, his future gone in an instant. Despite the fact that his parents had gotten off lightly, he knew without a doubt that he was now homeless. There was no way he could live with them.

Robin and Keith were thankfully absent, but Matthew found Rio in the basement playing video games. He probably hadn't moved from that spot in hours.

Matthew sank down on the sofa next to his friend.

"Hey," Rio greeted him, not taking his eyes from the screen. When Matthew didn't say anything, he finally looked over. "Jesus, what happened? You look like shit."

"My parents are criminals," Matthew said, tonelessly. "I lost my place at school."

Rio stared at him with a slightly open mouth. "That so?"

"I'm so fucked," Matthew said, picking at a thread on his jeans. "I don't even understand how it happened. What any of what my parents did has to do with me."

Rio was silent for a moment, then nodded. "Well, it's not the end of the world. You can come with me to Italy, and go pro, where you belong."

There was no sympathy, no care that Matthew had just had his life turned upside down. All Rio offered was a small smile. Rio was just being Rio, charming and self-centered, but a horrible suspicion crept up Matthew's spine as Rio offered him a small smile.

"It was you," he breathed.

"What?" Rio asked, brow furrowing in confusion.

Matthew shot up on the couch and rounded on Rio, almost tripping on the game controller's cord.

"How did DU find out about my parents?" he shouted, the disappointment and sadness igniting his temper like dry grass. "It's not like this was national fucking news, Rio. Someone must have tipped them off. Otherwise they'd have no idea!"

"You're going crazy, man," Rio said, with concern. "Calm down."

"It was you!" Matthew barreled on. "You're too scared to go to the pros alone! You need me next to you so you look good, so you threw me under the fucking bus so I couldn't go to college! You want me in your fucking shadow forever, is that it? So I can prop your ass up the rest of your fucking life?"

Rio surged to his feet and grabbed Matthew by the shirt. "If you say another word, I'll lay you out."

Matthew leaned in. "Fuck you, you fucking coward."

The pain that exploded in his jaw was almost welcome, something he could focus on instead of his cracking heart.

"Get out of my house," Rio growled, shoving Matthew toward the stairs. "And don't fucking come back until you're thinking clear."

Matthew took them two at a time and stumbled out the door. He nearly collided with Nicolette, who was just coming in.

"Whoa!" she said, grabbing onto his arm to steady herself. "Matthew! Hey!"

She beamed up at him. She'd recently gotten her braces removed and their absence made her look older.

"Hey," he mumbled, trying to get past her.

"Oh!" she cried, stepping further into his path. "What happened to your face?"

She laid cool fingers on his already sore jaw.

"Got in a fight with a tree," he said. It wasn't far from the truth.

She giggled, the carefree laugh of someone who knew she was loved. He couldn't help but smile at her.

"Here," she said, digging into her bag. She produced a small Tupperware and cracked it open. "This will help." She held something out, so he offered his palm.

She deposited a round cookie into his hand. It was slathered with smooth black icing and featured two crossed hockey sticks piped in red.

"I made them for Rio's going-away party, but I think you could use a cookie."

He stared at the symbol that had represented his life for so long, until the design grew blurry.

"Matthew?" Nicolette said, peering at him with a frown.

"See you around, Nic," he said, and practically pushed past her. When he was halfway down the street, he threw the cookie in a dumpster.

Everything had changed after that. There was no way it couldn't. He'd lost everything that mattered. He'd realized it the second Nicolette put that cookie in his hand. Her innocent gesture had given Matthew some resolve...he had to move on.

Matthew had always been pragmatic. Strong and reliable had always been his way and working hard held no fear for him. He moved out of his parents' house and had spent the next several months living on couches and in spare rooms. He worked odd jobs: busboy, construction, rideshare driver. The flexibility allowed him to get his real estate license. And brick by brick he built his life back up until he achieved some semblance of peace.

The tumbler of scotch was depressingly empty, and Matthew joined the Bad Decisions Club by pouring himself another helping.

Because the truth was, he wasn't at peace, and he certainly wasn't happy. He worked twelve-hour days, and he spent any down time he had at the gym. He'd dated for a while but despite his best intentions he couldn't find it in him to invest the time. After a while he figured that he just wasn't meant for a relationship. He assumed his business would sustain him or would at least gain him the respect and stability he craved.

He'd come to accept that this was it. A successful real estate empire would be his legacy. He didn't need anything else.

The thought kept him up most nights.

And now his carefully built life had been turned upside down. By locking away his pain, he'd also shut down his sense of joy, and now it all came gushing to the surface. The emotions swirling through him switched from anger to hope so fast he was getting dizzy. The scotch wasn't helping.

Though he knew that this situation with Rio would have affected him either way, there was another element contributing to the tilt in his equilibrium—Nicolette.

The bigger part of him wanted to cling to the safety of his life. How dare she tell him to let the past lie? Rio's betrayal had changed the entire course of his life, and his friend had gone on with his own life as if nothing had happened. What was there for her to "figure out"? He wasn't a project. As if she could just fix them like a broken glass, with some glue and elbow grease. Get Rio and Matthew to be friends again, like a fucking Hallmark movie.

Then there was the part he'd stifled for so long, the part that craved fun. And Nicolette was nothing if not fun. Her warmth and humor coupled with that zany sensibility drew him in like a fish on a line. His dick had a vested interest as well, his attraction an almost unfamiliar feeling after the months of drought.

But far more terrifying was that in just one kiss, Matthew had felt understood. Nicolette seemed to see through him. She had no idea what had happened but didn't seem ready to judge him for the possibilities. She'd known the boy that he used to be and recognized the man that he had always wanted to be. And accepted it all.

"Shit," Matthew whispered to the empty room.

He was in trouble.

Well and truly drunk, Matthew set his cup down and lay back, closing his eyes against the spinning room.

He wanted to focus on the hazy joy of the alcohol running through his veins, the simplicity of a kiss with a pretty girl.

But the wound was too deep. He'd worked too hard against all odds to simply let go, to forgive all the self-serving people who'd trampled him. It didn't matter that Rio was now the one dealing with a life halted. Yes, it was shitty, but it wasn't Matthew's problem.

He would never forget the life that Rio cost him, no matter how perfect Nicolette's lips tasted.

FIVE

The chipper ring of her cell phone stabbed Nicolette's brain into waking.

Everything ached and her already terrible vision had an extra layer of haze. Why did anyone think that drinking was a good idea?

Groaning, she fumbled for the offending device, sobering quickly when she saw her dad's name on the screen.

"Dad?" she asked tentatively. Though the doctors had assured them that Rio's life was not in danger, she knew how quickly things could change for the worse. Her heart skipped several beats, imagining every bad scenario.

"He's awake," her dad said, sounding so relieved it calmed Nicolette's beating heart. "Can you get here?"

Nicolette sat up, and immediately regretted it. Pain throbbed to life in her temple, the wine's last goodbye. "Yes," she said with a grimace. "Give me an hour."

"He asked for you," her dad said softly.

It took Nicolette a moment to swallow down the lump of feeling that had risen in her throat. Her brother was not the most demonstrative of people, fully owning his dude athlete persona. If he was asking for his little sister, things were serious.

"Is he... Does he know what happened?" Nicolette's voice cracked. The thought of Rio broken and alone in a hospital room felt like a knife in her side. And the questions about his ability to play hockey would inevitably occur to him. Every dream he'd ever had, dashed in the skid of a tire.

"More or less," her dad said. "The pain meds are keeping him in a pretty decent fog."

"Okay, Dad. I'll be there soon," Nicolette assured him.

She ended the call and threw on some comfortable clothes and her well-worn sneakers.

She fished a tote bag from her suitcase and proceeded to assemble a hospital kit: cell phone charger, e-reader, tissues, her toothbrush and toothpaste. On a whim she added some art supplies and paper. Maybe those kids would be there, and what kid didn't like to draw? Best be prepared. She might be at the hospital a while.

After freshening up, she made her way gingerly down the stairs. Her head pounded in protest, but she went straight to the living room to tell Matthew the good news.

And couldn't help the gasp that passed her lips.

Matthew was sprawled on the couch on his back, deep asleep, the morning light playing across his body in teasing strokes.

He was mouth-wateringly stunning. His gray T-shirt stretched tight across his chest, and his boxer briefs did nothing to conceal his strong thighs. She studiously ignored the very interesting bulge between them, instead focusing on his face.

Softened in sleep, his lips were slightly parted, and delicious stubble dusted his jaw. Well-defined eyebrows made him look serious even asleep, and Nicolette longed to brush his mussed hair from his forehead.

Her blood surged high as their kiss came back in sharp relief. That stubble had scoured the soft skin around her mouth. Those lips had tasted her with expert movements, opening her up in more ways than one. All that skin and heat, the pleasure that pooled between her legs from just a kiss.

It hadn't been just a kiss. Not really. Not for her.

He was everything she had ever dreamed of and yet nothing like her fantasy man. His churlish nature and the way he withheld himself were not what she would have expected from a mature Matthew. But that same steadiness was there, the same quiet warmth. If not for his tendency to be a jerk, Nicolette might have said she preferred Matthew as an adult.

Nicolette hesitated to wake him, almost wanting to let him sleep. Who knew what he would think about their kiss with the sun shining brightly through the curtains? Maybe it was best to indulge in the fantasy a little longer.

And then she caught sight of the bottle of scotch propped against the couch.

"Shit," she whispered. After all that wine, he'd gone for the liquor? Not a good sign. He was going to feel like the underside of a zookeeper's shoe.

Indeed, though she tried to be gentle waking him, he sat straight up with a thunderous expression on his face.

"What is it?" he rasped, wincing with what must be a headache to rival hers.

Nicolette handed him the glass of water she'd prepared for him, along with some painkillers.

"My dad just called. Rio's awake."

She waited for him to say something, but he just quietly sipped his water, eyes fixed on the wall behind her.

"I'm gonna head over there," she continued anyway, her temper rising along with her headache. "I thought I'd bring some stuff for those kids to keep them busy, but I also want to bring something for Rio. I have cookies but he probably won't want to eat much. I was thinking about bringing him one of his books just so he has something from home."

"Don't do that," Matthew said sharply, finally deciding to join the conversation.

"Don't do what?" Nicolette sniped. "Try to help my brother heal?"

The look that Matthew shot her made her throat dry up. The anger that burned in his blue eyes was potent, and though she was not the target, she'd never seen this side of Matthew. He'd always been so gentle.

"Not everyone treasures the past," he said with soft intensity. "You have to learn how to move on, or risk being a slave to what's happened."

Nicolette felt her anger answering his. "Really, Matthew? Like *you've* moved on? By letting go of everything that you ever cared about? How's that working for you?"

Matthew opened his mouth to respond, but Nicolette shook her head—a mistake, as her head violently protested.

"I don't want to argue," she said truthfully.

The prospect of getting into it with him was too much. Frustration made her want to grab him and shake him by the shoulders. He could philosophize about letting go on the one hand while stubbornly refusing to forgive what had happened to him. All of his experiences were not worth getting hung up on, except for the ones he chose. What a hypocrite.

And if he was so eager to live past-free, where did that leave them? Did every day get tossed into the bin when the sun went down? He was acting like their kiss had never happened. Maybe in his mind it hadn't. It had been as meaningless and uneventful—as easy to forget—as his years as part of her family.

She was far too hungover for this level of disappointment.

Because although she'd known better, a small part of her had hoped that the kiss meant as much to him as it did to her.

"Ugh!" she said, throwing up her hands. She went to the kitchen and began putting boxes of cookies in the bag.

A shadow in the kitchen entrance made her look, and there he stood, leaning against the frame like some modern-day Greek god. She wondered how hard he worked for those muscles, cursing her brain when an image of Matthew sweating and breathing had her own breath increasing.

She tried to ignore him, but he didn't budge. When she finally glanced up he was watching her with an amused smile.

"What?" she snarled.

He shrugged. "You clearly have more to say."

"I just don't get you!" she said immediately. "So many people have hard lives. But there are some who take the bad things that happened and make the best of them. Some even grow from them."

Nicolette knew she should stop while she was ahead, but as usual, once she'd started it was hard to stop.

"My boss in Denver, Luz, was homeless when she was a teenager. She managed to get a job as a custodian in a commercial kitchen. She said she always remembered her mom's *conchas* and wanted to learn how to bake. So she asked one of the bakers for help. She worked her way up and now she owns her own bakery. She uses some of her income to help homeless people get job training."

Matthew nodded. "That's pretty impressive."

"And my roommate, Rhoslyn," Nicolette barreled on. "Smartest woman I know. Was rejected by every university she applied to. So she decided to open her own boutique tea shop. It's small now but getting traction. She learned how to be a tea sommelier and makes her own blends."

Matthew studied her for a while. "You must miss them."

And that was enough for the tears to well. Yes, Chicago was her home, and she would do anything for her family. But Denver was her place too, and she had been building something, something that was *hers*. She felt torn in two, and guilty for even feeling that way.

"Right before the accident," she said, spurred on by the surprising kindness on his face, "I was planning on applying to do cookie art for Blue Hippo at a comic con."

"Blue Hippo?" Matthew asked with a smile.

She couldn't help but smile back. "They're an animation studio, movies for kids and stuff. The publicity if I got in would be amazing. I know I would get more jobs, and if I did well enough I could have my own bakery."

"Do it," Matthew said softly.

Nicolette cocked her head to the side. "What?"

"Apply. Do the con." He moved toward her a step and put a hand on her shoulder. "You're so talented, Nic. You could really do this. You deserve to do it."

He was brushing his hand over her shoulder, and his gaze dipped to her lips. Maybe he hadn't forgotten about their kiss after all.

But luckily Nicolette was made of sterner stuff. She moved away from him, putting the cookies in the tote bag. "I need to focus on what's in front of me right now. Rio deserves to have his family and *friends* supporting him."

"You're not being fair," Matthew growled, raking his hands through his already messy hair. "You make it sound so easy, but you have no idea what you're talking about. When have you ever had to face any hardships? Everybody has always loved you!"

The tote bag clattered to the ground, boxes of cookies spilling out across the kitchen floor. No doubt many of the cookies were broken, but Nicolette hardly cared. All she could see was red.

"My *mother* died," she hissed, poking him in the chest with her finger. "My father became a ghost of himself, and my brother disappeared entirely to live out some life of fame and celebrity. I've had to work my ass off to get through school and build my skillset to be competitive. Now my brother is in the hospital and I might have to give up on my own life for him. Don't you *dare* tell me I don't understand."

Matthew stood frozen, his eyes wide with shock and shame.

"Nicolette," he breathed. "Sweetheart, I..."

Before she knew what was happening he was tugging her into his arms, wrapping her against his strong body.

His scent filled her nose, pressed as it was against his collarbone, and she nearly got dizzy with it. She desperately wanted to sag against him, let him comfort her and tell her it would be all right.

"Rio doesn't deserve you," he said quietly.

"Deserve me?" Nicolette wriggled out of his hold and bent to gather the scattered boxes so she wouldn't have to look him in the eye. She was too pissed and hungover for this shit. "It's a good thing I don't think that the sun shines out of your ass anymore," Nicolette said. "I was so wrong about you. You act so wounded when all anyone wants is to be near you. You kiss me like you're drowning and then treat me like I'm your enemy. It's *you* Rio doesn't deserve."

"Nic—"

Her phone ringing cut him off, and Nicolette snatched it off the counter, grateful for the distraction.

She didn't recognize the number, but caution made her pick up.

"Hello?" she hazarded.

"Is this Nicolette?" a woman asked, the muted sound of a television in the background.

"Yes," Nicolette answered, drawing out the word.

The woman laughed. "Sorry to scare you. My name is Mora. We met at the hospital yesterday? My husband is André from the Guardians?"

"Oh yeah! Hey! I was just thinking about you this morning. I was going to bring some stuff for your kids."

"That's so sweet," Mora gushed. "Listen, I got your number from your dad and he mentioned that you don't have a car at the moment. I'm on my way back to the hospital. Do you need a ride?"

Nicolette nearly fell to her knees in gratitude. Matthew was hovering nearby like a specter, and her confusion about him was too overwhelming. She needed to take a page from his book and just leave.

"Yes, that would be amazing," Nicolette replied, accidentally catching Matthew's eyes. They'd already shuttered, reverted back to that benign mask he showed the world. Somehow, that hurt her most of all, now that she knew what he could really be.

"Great!" Mora said. "Just text me your address."

They hung up and Nicolette sent her address before adding Mora as a contact.

"If you give me a minute to wash up, I'll take you to the hospital," Matthew was saying, heading back toward the living room.

"No need," Nicolette said, shouldering her bag. "That was the woman from the hospital yesterday. She offered me a ride." She offered him a sweet smile. "See? No need to be involved any further."

She brushed past him, knowing she was being a bitch. But she wanted to hurt him, like he'd hurt her.

He grabbed her hand as she went past, his grip gentle but fervent.

"That's not what I want," he said, sounding surprised at his own words.

But Nicolette shook her head. "Yes, it is. You have your own life to get on with. We'll be fine without you."

She pulled from his grasp and went to the door.

"I'm going to wait on the porch. You can stay as long as you like. Just lock the door behind you. Unless you don't remember where Dad hides the key."

"Nicolette," he said, voice low with some emotion she couldn't name. But it made her pause, facing the street through the frame of the door.

"I don't do what I do to hurt anyone," he said slowly. "To hurt you."

His footsteps approached and his body heat tickled the back of her neck. Her eyes drifted closed and she knew if she leaned back, she would fall into him.

"I do it to protect myself," he admitted, his voice next to her ear. "I do it because I learned the hard way that some people are *not* what they seem."

Nicolette stiffened. He meant Rio. He might even have meant her.

"Drive safe," she said, and went out, slamming the door behind her.

On the porch, Nicolette breathed deep, trying not to think about the infuriating man in her house. She wasn't angry anymore, just sad.

She hated to admit it, but Matthew had touched a nerve. How much was she willing to give up no matter how desperately she loved her family? A more terrifying thought was that despite their inability to see eye to eye, Nicolette suspected that her heart was in far deeper with Matthew than she cared to admit.

~

MATTHEW WATCHED from the window as Nicolette climbed into a blue minivan. It sped off trailing exhaust and a sense of finality. The last twenty-four hours had been exhilarating and exhausting. He'd even felt a tiny spark of hope with Nicolette last night, that at last he had found his place.

As usual, he was reminded that he was not built for hope. Only for work and survival. Nicolette had reminded him of that. He couldn't be the person she wanted him to be. And he would move on and find a way to be okay with that.

He dressed slowly, his head sending rays of pain to the rest of his body. He replaced the scotch on the bookshelf and folded the blanket, running his hands over the colorful threads.

Robin always had a crochet hook in her hands it seemed, making blankets and sweaters for anyone who needed them— and those who didn't.

One Christmas she'd slaved over two elaborate matching scarves, which she'd given to him for his parents.

He'd screwed up his face in disgust. "Why are you giving *them* anything?"

She'd sighed, like she always sighed with him. "I know you don't get along with them, Matthew. But they care, in their way. You have to find it in you to forgive them. Sometimes when you accept people for what they are, you don't need to be angry about what they are not."

The Nicolette apple had not fallen far from the Robin tree.

He drove home, relishing the breeze on his face, glad to leave behind that haunted home once and for all.

Once home, he took a long shower, turned up as hot as he

could stand. His hope was to purge the alcohol from his body, sweat it all out. Maybe he could purge Nicolette too.

But she remained, like a brand on his skin, and once he'd put on clean clothes, he had no idea what to do with himself.

Work wasn't an option. It was too late already and he was far too hungover. Maybe he could just crawl into bed and hope for the bliss of oblivion. Or do what he really wanted to do—think about Nicolette, find a way through what she'd told him. If only she could understand...

His phone buzzed. It was Austin.

"Are you bringing Nic to the hospital?" his friend asked.

"Hi, Austin, I'm good, how are you?" Matthew said brightly, flopping down on his sofa.

"Cut the shit, man," Austin said brusquely. "Where are you guys?"

"Nicolette's friend from the waiting room picked her up about thirty minutes ago," Matthew explained.

"Damn it," Austin mumbled. "Okay, well you need to get down here. Rio's awake."

"I know," Matthew muttered.

"It's bad, Matthew. He knows what his prognosis is and... I've never seen him like this."

Matthew sat up a little straighter. Austin was the easygoing, unruffled one of their trio, always upbeat. To hear his voice crack with emotion was alarming. Matthew couldn't help but ask. "What's his condition?"

There was a long pause, and Matthew could hear his pulse thrumming in his ears.

"Surgery was successful, but his leg..." Austin finally said quickly, as if to get it out of the way. "He has at least a year of rehab and healing ahead. Maybe more surgeries. They aren't saying anything for sure, but it's pretty likely his hockey career is done."

Matthew had been angry for a long time about the loss of his own hockey career. Rio had been the focal point of that anger, fueled by Rio's meteoric rise to stardom. The irony of Rio's condition was not lost on him, and some deep, desperate part of him wanted to gloat.

But he couldn't. He could only imagine half of what Rio was going through. It wasn't just the game that had been torn from him, but his strong body. Matthew felt tired and helpless in the face of so much loss.

"You have to be here," Austin was saying.

"What?" Matthew asked, as if he hadn't heard the request. Yes, he felt awful for Rio, but that didn't wipe away what had happened. Why was everyone so insistent that *he* was the key to Rio's recovery?

"Rio is going to need us more than ever," Austin continued, ignoring Matthew's terse response. "It's not just the physical therapy and everything. He's not taking it well. They have him on all these drugs, but...he knows. He knows what this means."

"I don't see what that has to do with me," Matthew said, knowing he sounded like a petulant child.

"Jesus Christ, you are such a dick!" Austin exploded, and Matthew cringed at the strain in his friend's voice. "We are brothers, no matter what you think happened in the past!"

"I—" Matthew started, but Austin was having none of it.

"Hockey is over now, for all of us. It's just us now. This is real, Matthew, not a game. This is the rest of our lives. And Rio is going to need you by his side."

"Like he was by my side when I lost my scholarship?" he spat. God, he felt like the broken record of a bitter old man. But he couldn't just let it go, even for Austin. He'd built this wall brick by dusty brick. It was too well constructed to just knock down.

"What the hell are you talking about?" Austin asked, something sharp in his tone.

Matthew realized his friend had been waiting for this opening for a long time, and the thought of revealing everything that had happened was terrifying. He realized that he wasn't really sure Austin would understand.

"Nothing," Matthew mumbled. "But I'm not coming. If you want to pretend that the past never happened, that's great. But Rio had his chance. I'm sorry it ended this way, but he's had a career. I never got that chance. He took mine from me."

"Dude, throw me a bone here," Austin said, frustration creeping into his tone. "What the fuck are you talking about?"

"Forget about it," Matthew said, wanting to kick himself for saying anything at all. These last few days must have addled his brain. All this reminiscing and his need to confess was like a burning ember on the tip of his tongue. He had a dire need to spit it out and find relief.

"Whatever," Austin said, voice laden with disappointment. "Nicolette's here. I'll talk to you later."

He disconnected the call without another word.

Luckily, the phone rang almost immediately, saving Matthew from turning the conversation over in his mind.

It was Chris, his contractor.

"Hey, Matthew," Chris's gravelly voice greeted him.

"Chris, what's up?" Matthew said, trying to sound unruffled. "Everything at the site okay?"

"Yeah, I have some news about that, but I wanted to ask if you were okay?"

"What do you mean?" Matthew asked, mystified.

"I saw on the news about Rio Hayes. They said the injuries are serious. I was just calling to check in."

For fuck's sake, would his life forever be about Rio? The man was like a black hole, sucking in everything around him until they were consumed. Even Chris, whom Matthew had kept at a distance like everyone in his life, was dazzled by Rio's light. And he'd never even met him.

"Um, yeah, I just got the news this morning," Matthew said. "It seems like this might end his career."

"Shit, that's terrible," Chris said with some heat. "Believe it or not, I saw you two play a couple of times." There was a smile in Chris's voice as he continued. "My brother played in high school, so your teams met up. I remember you and Rio mucking around on the bench."

Yeah, while they'd been serious about hockey, even the brief downtime on the bench was an opportunity for antics, much to their coach's consternation. That coach coined their name, the Terrible Trio, always spoken with a resigned smile. Despite liking to keep his nose clean, Rio had always pulled Matthew into their shenanigans.

"Is he doing okay?" Chris was asking. "This can't be easy."

Matthew was slightly taken aback. Chris had no reason to care about him or Rio outside of his business with Matthew. That the man had taken the time to call was touching and a little humbling.

"I'm not sure," Matthew admitted. "I haven't seen him."

He spoke the truth without revealing to Chris that this was by choice. He didn't want to disappoint the other man or make him think that Matthew was an asshole. What kind a of a person abandoned a friend, after all? Chris didn't know what kind of man Rio had been. He couldn't know that what Rio had done to Matthew that could never be undone. That was far too much to even begin to bring into this conversation.

"Well, take care, man. This kind of thing can be exhausting."

"Thanks," Matthew said. "You said you had some news about the site."

"Oh, right," Chris said, all business now. "You can actually take your time to reschedule the inspection. We hit a little snag in the demo, found something that looks like asbestos tile under the carpet. So now we have to wait for an asbestos abatement contractor."

"Shit," Matthew said, glad that Chris was on the up and up, but annoyed at the pause this would put in his plans.

"Yeah, well, it's not a huge deal," Chris continued. "But we want to do this right. My dad built this company and so it's my reputation as well as my guys' health at risk. But I'll keep you updated."

They hung up after a few more pleasantries, and Matthew immediately reached for the remote. Flicking the channels until he reached the sports news, he stared in shock at the screen.

Splashed across the bottom in bold letters was the breaking news story: RIO HAYES, STAR FORWARD OF THE INDI-ANAPOLIS GUARDIANS, CAREER OVER AFTER TEAM BUS CRASH.

They sure didn't mince words, but Matthew hardly noticed that. What caught his attention was the camera zooming in on a crowed outside of the doors to the recovery suite. The view was from the side, the profiles of the security team stern.

And there was Nicolette pushing through the crowed. She stumbled a few times, almost losing hold of her bag. No one steadied her, or even moved aside so she could pass easily.

But the worst part was her face, pale and tight with worry, her eyes red under her glasses. And she was about to go through those doors and hear the news.

This feed must have been old, because Austin had said she'd already arrived. So she already knew.

He wondered how she was handling it. Probably by taking care of everyone else, passing around cookies and hugs for everyone who needed it. Holding Rio's hand and stroking his hair and letting him believe that everything would be okay.

But who was taking care of her?

Matthew shot up from the couch and grabbed his keys. Austin would need him. And Keith. He should really be there, at least for them.

He deflated like a balloon poked with a pin. He was usually so certain about things. He could make business decisions in a snap. It was one of the things people working with him liked. No-nonsense and honest. There was no waffling with Matthew Collins.

And he had no idea what he was supposed to do. Sit here worrying about the people he cared about? Or go to them and be forced to face the man who'd stolen his future?

The sofa was not as comfortable as the Hayes's but it felt like heaven to his sore body. He couldn't go, he decided, but maybe he could connect with *someone* he cared about.

For the third time in an hour, he picked up his phone and pressed a contact.

"Matthew!" Shelby answered on the third ring. "What's wrong?"

She sounded worried and rightfully so. When Matthew had distanced himself from his parents, his siblings had been collateral damage. He still spoke to them, but very seldom. He hadn't seen Jackson in person in a few years.

"Nothing's wrong, Shelby," Matthew said, trying to sound reassuring. "I just wanted to talk to my baby sister."

"Okay," she said, still sounding skeptical.

"How are you?" he asked breezily. "How's school going?"

"I'm fine. School's good, but I seem to have to work ten times harder than anyone else. That's being homeschooled by Mom and Dad for you."

"But you're keeping up?" he asked.

"Give me some credit, Matthew. I'm not an idiot." She sounded a little angry and he realized he'd struck a nerve.

"No, you're not. The Collins kids are all known for their smarts."

She snorted. "I don't know. Jackson makes me wonder sometimes."

"How is he?" Matthew asked, feeling a little guilty. Maybe if he'd stuck around, Jackson wouldn't have turned out to be such a wild child. Another casualty of his parents' betrayal.

"The same," Shelby said. "He texts completely in pictures, and from what I can tell, he's not exactly living slow."

"And, um, Mom and Dad?" The question slipped out before he could stop himself.

There was a long pause on the other end of the line.

"Matthew, what's really going on?" she asked, sounding impatient.

"See? And you thought you weren't smart." He huffed a laugh, hoping to distract her.

It didn't work. "I'd like to remind you that *you* called *me*. So spill."

"Have you seen the news about Rio Hayes?" he asked.

"No," she said hesitantly. "What happened?"

"Look him up," Matthew said, too tired of running the details over to explain them.

He heard the clacking of computer keys, and then her gasp into the phone.

"Oh, no!" she cried. "Oh, Matthew, how awful."

"He's here, in Chicago," he said, wondering why he was telling her this.

The inevitable question came. "Have you seen him?"

"No. But I've seen Nicolette."

"She must be beside herself," Shelby said with sympathy. "Send her my love when you see her."

"Shelby, I—"

"I'm going to send a card. Can you tell me Rio's room number?"

Matthew pulled up Austin's text with the info and relayed it to her.

"Thanks," she said. "Do you need anything?"

"Why would I need anything?"

He could practically hear Shelby rolling her eyes. "Because your estranged best friend just had his legs mangled in an accident and you're asking about Mom and Dad. Just those little things."

Matthew hesitated. Rio and his parents were the last things he wanted to talk about. But Shelby did have information that he wanted.

"What do you remember about Nicolette from when she babysat you?" he asked, hoping he didn't sound too eager.

"She was fun," Shelby said. "We were always drawing or doing crafts and stuff. I was always jealous of her style."

Matthew almost laughed. Could Nic's look be called a style? She was more like an exclamation.

"But she always seemed a little lost," Shelby continued.

"What do you mean?" Matthew asked.

"Well, she didn't have many friends. And everyone was so focused on Rio. Her dad was a workaholic. So it was really just her and her mom."

And then Robin had died. He remembered saying that she didn't understand and felt a fresh wave of guilt. Everything he'd ever thought about this family had been turned on its head and he wasn't sure what he needed to do to make sense of it.

"Why are you asking about her?" Shelby asked coyly.

"Because...I just remembered her differently," he answered honestly. Shelby didn't need the whole picture.

"People change, Matthew," Shelby said sagely. "It's both the wonderful and the terrible thing about time passing."

"Have you been reading those self-help books again?" Matthew teased to cover how true those words rang.

"Hey, at least I am improving myself. My brothers could do with a little personal reflection. And not the type you get by checking out a mirror."

"Fair enough," he said with a grin.

"How's Austin taking all this?" she asked.

That question gave Matthew pause. Was there more than one childhood crush simmering under the surface of the present? "He's, you know...Austin. Why do you ask?" Matthew tried to keep the teasing from his voice.

"Shut it," Shelby said. "Austin was always the sweetest of the three of you. I'm sure he's running around like a chicken with his head off trying to make sure everyone's where they need to be."

"You know him well," Matthew said.

"Hey," she said softly. "This was nice. Maybe we could do this keeping-in-touch thing more often?"

The hope in her voice made him feel hopeful in return. Maybe some broken things could be fixed—or at least mended.

"Sure, kid. I'd like that."

SIX

"He needs his rest," the doctor said. "He's on some very strong painkillers, so his responsiveness may be low."

Nicolette's dad nodded, then put his hand on her lower back, pushing her into Rio's room ahead of him.

A brief flash of nerves shot through her. Her dad should have been leading the way, creating a buffer between her and the upset that lay ahead. That was a parent's job—to protect their children even in the face of their own pain. But her dad had always been this way, and she'd let him be. Being the reliable one was her choice, her role. And she didn't run from it now. She set her face into an expression of loving calm and braced herself to see her brother—and to handle whatever, and she did mean whatever, she needed to. For him. For her dad. For all of them.

Every bit of nerves evaporated when she saw Rio. They'd propped him up and his thin hospital blankets were neatly tucked at his waist. His head lolled back against the pillows, his eyes half lidded. He looked so small and vulnerable, nothing like her boisterous, troublesome, bright brother. Even his body under the blankets looked smaller than the hulking, powerful athlete's she remembered. Surely he couldn't have changed...it was the circumstances that made even the most strong humans seem fragile. Humbled.

Nicolette took a few unsteady steps forward, and nearly stopped short again. There were charge notes on the wall in bold dry erase markers. Names of nurses and instructions were highlighted with colorful arrows and circles. Monitors and IVs and equipment dinged, creating a noisy, almost impossibly boisterous environment. So much equipment. How the hell could her brother recover, rest, with all of this?

But even as Nic took it all in, she knew. She understood. This was real injury, real illness. This was Rio's reality now. No more plush hotel rooms and swanky California king beds to rest his frazzled body after a night of intense play. He was confined to a narrow, plastic bed. His only company he'd have —his patient care team. His only music—the discordant notes of the machines that did their work to keep him hydrated, medicated, and monitored. Tears stung Nic's eyes but she blinked them back, grateful as hell her brother was still here. Their mother hadn't been as lucky...as if *luck* was what they had to blame for losing her.

A soft moan escaped Rio's lips and jostled Nic from her shocked inventory of the room. She finally crossed to his side, choosing the side of the bed with the fewest wires and lines to interrupt. She gently took his hand, trying to avoid looking at the harsh bruises that dotted his arms and face. She'd known his legs had been injured, but it hadn't occurred to her that his entire body had been jostled, damaged in the crash. His face showed signs of being smashed around—not the joyful, intentional blows of a passionate on-ice fight. But a one-man battle against metal that Rio looked like he'd lost. Badly.

"Rio?" she asked softly, keeping her voice still and calm. Even if Rio didn't need her to fight the tears, she knew if she let them come, there would be no stopping them. "Can you hear me?"

He turned his head slowly, and he stared unfocused at her for a few heart-stopping moments.

And then he whispered, "Nic?"

The painful knot of tears she'd been holding back broke through, pouring down her face. She squeezed his hand and brushed his hair back from his face.

"I'm here," was all she could manage.

To her concern, Rio started crying himself, great hiccupping sobs as he clutched her hand.

"It hurts, Nic," he croaked.

He was too weak to go on, and Nicolette tried to calm him down, making soothing sounds.

She had naively thought that once they knew Rio was going to live, they would be able to deal with the rest as it came. But her brother's whole life had been hockey. His entire identity was playing center ice. Hell, she didn't even know if he'd ever had any friends who weren't somehow connected to the game.

With that gone, there was so much more than just his legs to worry about. It wasn't just a question of what Rio would do now that he couldn't play. Who would Rio Hayes be if he didn't play hockey?

Even in his drugged-up state, Rio seemed to understand this. Nicolette had never seen her brother cry. Through every injury and setback, he'd remained the same cocky, goofy self. Nothing ever fazed him, because what could upset someone so blessed?

His tears terrified her. She would do anything to help him, but at that moment, she had no idea what to do.

A warm hand squeezed her shoulder, and she looked up to

see her dad standing beside her, Austin hovering by the door. Her dad offered her a tissue and a small smile.

"It's okay, kiddo," he whispered, whether to her or Rio she wasn't sure. But it didn't really matter. He was there, really there, and it brought on fresh tears.

Despite her previous vow to be the rock for her family to stand on, Nicolette realized that they were in this together. Though she would do everything she could for her brother, she wouldn't be alone. The thought made her feel stronger than she had in years.

"Nic," Rio whispered again.

"Shh," she soothed, wiping his face with the tissue. "Try not to talk. You have to rest so you can heal. And Dad and Austin and I will be here every step of the way. Whatever you need, you big jerk. I love you," she said, tucking the blanket around him more securely.

"You too," he slurred, his eyes drooping shut.

Nicolette stared down at him for another minute, just feeling grateful that he was here. When she turned away, Austin had approached.

"Hey," he said, wrapping her in a hug.

"Hey yourself," she said, trying to lighten the heavy atmosphere in the room.

Austin hugged her dad.

"Thanks for coming, son," Keith said, patting Austin's back before releasing him.

"I can't stay long," Austin said, looking unhappy. "Gotta get back to the diner. I've called in favors with every cousin I have to cover for me, and I've run out of cousins."

They laughed, the action feeling so good that Nicolette could have kissed him.

"You didn't have to do that," she said instead, thinking of Matthew unwilling to even set foot in the hospital.

Austin gave her a sad smile, as if he knew exactly what she was thinking. "You know I do. You guys always took care of me. It's my turn now."

They paused to get well and truly emotional all over again, her dad surreptitiously wiping his eyes.

"Anyway," Austin continued. "I should be able to sneak away for a bit every day, but Mom really needs me tonight."

"Of course," Nicolette said.

"When you guys finish up here, you should come by the diner," Austin said. "Mom said she has some stuff for you, and I think you guys could use a good meal."

"Sounds great," her dad said. A look of confusion crossed her father's face then. "Is Matthew going to come soon?"

"Matthew?" came the weak voice from behind them. They turned to see Rio struggling to open his eyes. "Matthew's here? I want to see him..."

Nicolette bit her lip hard, wondering what god she had pissed off to deserve this. His whole family was there and Rio grew the most excited at the prospect of seeing Matthew. Even now Rio was struggling to keep his eyes open and glancing around the room, as if Matthew was there, waiting to surprise him.

She didn't get it at all. How could Matthew fight against seeing Rio, based on some perceived past slight, while Rio wanted nothing more than to see his friend, even while doped up and not entirely sure what was going on?

Was it jealousy? Maybe Matthew had not been able to go pro and couldn't stomach it that Rio had and they'd fallen out.

No, that didn't seem right. The three had always been a team, and they'd always rallied around Rio as the one who had the skills to make it. That had been no secret.

There had to be more to it than that.

A woman?

A hazy memory snapped into focus. It was right before Matthew had disappeared, and Rio had brought a woman home to hang out with them.

That wasn't strictly allowed, but her parents had been out and with Rio leaving soon, rules tended to be overlooked.

"This is Lila," Rio said, his arm wrapped securely around the girl's tiny waist. Everything about her was tiny, and teenage Nicolette was both jealous of and fascinated by this perfect example of womanhood. Her long brown hair was in perfect messy waves; her immaculate makeup made her big eyes pop. The outfit she sported, though barely there, looked like something out of a catalogue for teenage influencers.

Nicolette had smoothed her own frizzy hair down and had tried to stay out of the line of site, sitting on the bottom steps.

Lila watched the boys play video games, clapping in delight and pouting at appropriate intervals. She was all over Rio. Stroking his arm and even nuzzling his ear, murmuring things that Nicolette was grateful not to hear.

But Matthew had seemed to notice. He stole glances when he thought no one was looking.

So this was the kind of girl that Matthew liked, Nicolette had thought glumly. She couldn't even bring herself to be jealous. All she felt was despair that this was just one more reason why Matthew would never be hers.

Around midnight, Rio stood up, handing his controller to Lila.

"Gotta make a beer run. My contact is waiting." He made it sound far more illicit than it was. Their cousin Simon would get them booze on the condition that he got free hockey tickets and that it didn't come back on him. Simon's house was about ten minutes away.

He and Austin left, leaving Matthew and Lila on opposite ends of the couch. Not a minute had passed before Lila scooted across the couch. Nicolette watched in fascinated horror as the girl pulled Matthew's controller from his hand and climbed boldly into his lap.

"What are you doing?" Matthew said, staring up at Lila's smiling face.

"What does it feel like?" she crooned, running her fingers down Matthew's bicep.

"I can't—" Matthew said, trying to push her off, but Lila was stronger than she looked and clung to him.

They'd obviously forgotten that Nicolette was there, and she was not about to stick around to see Matthew put his mouth on anyone.

The memory had gotten lost in the tumult of life, but what if Lila had been playing both boys? What if Rio had chosen her over Matthew? Maybe she had been Matthew's first love and Rio had betrayed their friendship over a pretty pair of green eyes...

"Nicolette!" someone hissed. It was her dad, holding Rio's hand as he murmured "Matthew, Matthew," over and over.

Austin gave her a funny look. She must have really checked out, but she still didn't know what to tell Rio. She didn't want to lie, but she also did not want to upset him with the truth. Matthew wasn't coming.

Austin apparently had no such qualms, and he bent the truth to breaking. "Matthew's really busy, Rio. You know he's a big-shot real estate guy. But he helped us by picking Nicolette up at the airport. Took good care of your baby sister."

If only they know how much. Nicolette tamped down a blush as Austin continued.

"But now you got to rest, okay, man? And maybe Matthew can make some time to see you soon."

This seemed to placate Rio and he settled back, closing his eyes. Soon his breathing grew deep and even. Nicolette heaved a sigh of relief, feeling like she'd dodged a bullet. Of course, it would only last until Rio got worked up again. Somehow she knew that there was going to be a reckoning of some kind, and she could only pray she wasn't caught in the crosshairs.

The doctor came again and told them Rio needed his rest.

"When you come next time we will discuss a treatment and recovery plan," she said, smiling kindly. "Rio has a long way to go."

They filed out into the hallway. Nicolette hated the thought of Rio here alone, disoriented and in pain. Exhaustion settled on her and she had to keep herself from swaying on her feet. There was no way she would look weak in front of her dad right now. He had enough to worry about.

Instead she smiled brightly. "Should we head to Austin's now, Dad? I've literally had nothing to eat."

"Nicolette!" her dad scolded, but he acquiesced, looking like he could use a meal himself.

"Do you mind if I ride with Austin?" she asked, hoping her dad wouldn't be offended. She had questions burning holes in her brain and she was going to burst if she didn't get answers soon.

"Of course not, sweetheart," her dad said, kissing the top of her head. "First one there buys the pie."

Austin knew her well enough not to make her wait. "Okay, what's going on, short stack?"

"Short stack?" she laughed. Austin hadn't called her that for years.

The smile melted from his face. "Seeing Rio like that, it just makes me think of when we were little. I dunno. Too nostalgic. Fuck." He sighed the last word and Nicolette nodded in understanding.

"So what do you want to know?" Austin said, eyes on the road.

"Did Matthew and Rio have a falling out over a woman?" Nicolette asked, not bothering to beat around the bush.

Austin started laughing, so much it devolved in coughs, and Nicolette felt a little foolish.

"What?" she demanded.

Austin wiped his eyes with the back of his hand. "Rio and Matthew have very different tastes in women. If they ever argued over a girl, it was to convince the other that she was hot."

Men were such mystifying creatures. But maybe that was why all this had happened.

"What about Lila?" Nicolette asked, urging Austin to have the answers.

"Who?" he said, throwing her a confused glance.

"There was this girl, long brown hair, Rio brought her home once and she and Matthew..." She trailed off. She didn't actually know what she and Matthew had gotten up to, but she could guess.

"Oh," Austin said, going a little quiet. "Yeah, I remember her. Lila Curran. They *did* get into a fight about her."

Hah, Nicolette thought, with a sick sort of triumph.

"It's not what you're thinking," Austin sighed with a little grin. "Lila was huge into sports. She actually started a club hockey league for girls when she realized there was no hockey team that would let girls play. Rio was trying to set Matthew up with Lila. He thought they'd be perfect together but Matthew didn't like it. He said he didn't want Rio's castoffs, that Rio thought he couldn't even get his own girlfriend without Rio's help. But they made up."

While she'd been wrong about the situation, this answer unlocked another piece of the Matthew puzzle. She'd always thought the three of them rode their popularity equally, reaping the benefits of being young and somewhat famous.

But if Rio thought Matthew needed help, and Matthew resented that help...

He was shy, she realized. And maybe a little self-conscious. She knew what a personality Rio was. He'd drag people in his wake if he wasn't careful. It was suddenly clear to her how Matthew might have gotten lost in Rio's glow.

But was that enough to sever such a close relationship?

"So what happened?" Nicolette groaned in frustration. "Rio seems to love Matthew and Matthew wants nothing to do with him. You guys were inseparable. What happened?"

Austin stared out of the windshield with an intensity that would melt glass. He seemed to be turning something over in his mind.

"If I could, it's not my story to tell, Nic."

And that was it. No further explanation or hint. And Nicolette knew better than to pry. Austin was one of those guys who valued loyalty. And Matthew came before Nicolette's curiosity.

"Just be careful, Nic," he said as they pulled into the diner parking lot.

"What do you mean?" she asked, unbuckling her seatbelt.

He paused with his hands still on the steering wheel. "It's not your job to fix things. I don't want you to get hurt because you want to heal everyone. They'll figure it out. Or they won't. It's not on you."

Nicolette shifted uncomfortably in her seat. What was it with her being surrounded by people who were too astute by half?

"I just want to get Rio in a good place," she said. "Then we can worry about everything else."

It was mostly the truth, and Austin seemed to accept it. He jerked his thumb at the silver sedan parked next to them.

"Your dad beat us," he laughed. "Guess pie's on us. Dutch apple today."

He came around to Nicolette's side and helped her out of the car.

"Thursdays are the best here," he said, opening the diner door for her. "My favorite regulars come in."

She laughed. "I don't come here enough to know the regulars."

Austin shrugged, winked, and turned to greet her dad, waiting by the counter.

~

"HEY, HANDSOME," Austin's mom, Yvette, greeted him with a wink. "Coffee?"

Matthew was tucked into his favorite booth at The Finer Diner, a nearly famous local business that Austin's mother had built and maintained with nothing but her own two hands and a lot of love. The place had started out as a 1950s throwback, complete with exposed stone walls and red leatherette booths, but over the years, Yvette had restored the place and changed the décor to reflect a classic art deco sensibility.

"People love a dive," Yvette had explained to Matthew once. "But they also don't want their asses to stick to the booth."

Yvette kept a clean shop and served food that bordered on gourmet. It had been a wonderland when he was a kid and offered unlimited mashed potatoes. Home-cooked meals had been few and far between at his house.

Ever since he could remember, every Thursday Matthew had come to The Finer Diner to shoot the shit with Yvette and some of Austin's cousins. All the Ames kids ended up here at some point, working summer jobs or to pick up quick cash after school. Yvette tried to pretend that she could do everything from hostess to line cook, but she was always thrilled to bring in young fresh help. She'd never been known to turn away someone in need of a job—even, for a very short time after high school, Matthew himself.

Matthew had warm memories of the days he'd bussed tables under the watchful eye of Yvette. All these years later, he loved coming here and feeling that camaraderie. Yvette was another of his adopted parents. Unlike Robin with her gentle optimism, Yvette tended to be a little coarser in her kindness. He supposed that came from working as hard as she had, and he liked her no less for it.

"Hey, Yvette," he said, giving her the full-wattage smile.

She pretended to swoon. "Honey, you have to be careful with that thing. You're gonna cause car crashes."

He laughed at the old joke between them. "I'll pay for the damages."

She poured him a full cup of coffee. "You came just in time. Austin is on his way back from the hospital."

This was news to Matthew. He almost hadn't come, figuring he'd avoid Austin and any new tasks he would demand of Matthew.

"I wouldn't have asked him to leave Rio," Yvette was saying. "But we're swamped."

Matthew breathed a small sigh of relief. If Austin was working he'd be able to eat and sneak away without the guilt trip.

"This whole thing is so messed up," Yvette said suddenly, and Matthew was horrified to see tears in her eyes. "One moment and Rio's whole life is changed."

She got quiet and Matthew knew she was thinking about Austin, about her own son, in that situation. He wanted to assure her that it would be okay, that if there was anyone who could pull through, it was Rio.

But he didn't know. He couldn't comfort her—not about Rio. He'd made that choice, and he would stick to it.

Yvette shook her melancholy off and grinned at him. "As much as I like talking with my favorite son, work beckons. Order?"

He asked for spaghetti and meatballs, craving the comforting carbs.

Once Yvette walked away, Matthew pulled out his phone, fingers hovering over the search bar. He didn't want to know, not really. But something made him type "Indianapolis Guardians" into the search box.

His search feed flooded with images and articles. He clicked on the first one and began to read.

The jingle of the door made Matthew glance up. Keith Hayes had walked in the door, followed shortly by Nicolette and Austin.

Keith spotted Matthew immediately and made a beeline to the booth. Matthew shoved his phone in his pocket and put what he hoped was a pleasant look on his face.

"Matthew!" Keith said, taking Matthew by the shoulder. "We missed you at the hospital. Rio's awake! He even asked for you."

Matthew cut his gaze to Austin, who had approached as well. Austin gave a tiny shrug, his expression revealing nothing.

"Hey, I got to get to work," Austin announced before the conversation could go much further. "I'll be back at the hospital tomorrow, though. See you, Matthew."

The words were laden with meaning, and Matthew stared holes into Austin's retreating back.

"So..." Nic stammered.

Nicolette. He'd noticed her as soon as they'd walked in. In a blue dress and leggings, her sneakers a sunny yellow, she was the brightest thing in the room. She'd tied her hair up into a loose bun, and errant tendrils had escaped to caress her soft-looking neck.

What he would give to taste the skin there. Pull her soft hair from its confines and dig his hands into it, pull her body against his. He would escape into her, find the most joyful oblivion with her.

"Can we sit here?"

He snapped back from his ridiculous fantasy. There would never be uncomplicated *anything* with Nicolette Hayes.

He could hardly refuse, so he waved to the bench across from him.

They scooted in, and despite Matthew's rhapsodizing about Nicolette, up close, they both looked like shit. Faces drawn and eyes tired, they practically sagged in the booth.

One of Austin's many cousins, Bree, a miniscule slip of a waitress, came to take their order.

"Hi," she said, her sandy blond braid hanging over a shoulder. After she took their orders she delivered a message from her boss. "Yvette has food packaged for you to take home. Don't forget it when you leave."

This caused Keith to tear up a bit and Nicolette stroked her dad's arm as she thanked Bree.

Though he had no right and was afraid he might be opening up a can of worms, Matthew asked the question that burned against his heart. "So how are you? How did...um, how was the day?"

Nicolette opened her mouth to answer but Keith got there first. "I thought once he woke up it would be easier," he said, talking to his hands folded on the table. "That this nightmare would be over. But I feel like my son is gone forever."

"Dad," Nicolette breathed, looking stricken. Matthew realized that she still expected her dad to be the strong one, even though he'd never been the same after Robin died.

Keith's whole body seemed to sag then, and he ran a hand across his eyes.

"Hey, kiddo," he rasped. "I'm so tired all of a sudden. Do you think that Matthew can drive you home? I'd like to go."

"But we haven't eaten!" Nicolette protested half-heartedly, her dad already standing. "And I'm sure Matthew has plans."

"No, it's fine," Matthew said truthfully. They looked so *hurt*. At that moment he would have done anything for them. For her.

"Thank you, son," Keith said to Matthew. He caressed Nicolette's head. "You get some food in you, baby. I'll see you at home."

He walked out of the restaurant, leaving them alone.

Nicolette sat, gaze in her lap, looking so vulnerable he felt an answering ache. She bit her full lower lip, and he wanted to cross over to her and sooth that sting. All that sweet energy she trailed in her wake was dampened and he hated that he'd had a hand in it.

"Um," she started, still not looking at him.

"We don't have to talk," Matthew assured softly.

This made her look up, surprise evident in her green eyes.

"You've had a long day," he said, hoping he sounded more supportive than desperate. Desperate to *not* talk. "Talking isn't important," he said with a casual shrug.

She nodded slowly, then rummaged through her ridiculous yellow bag and pulled out a sketchbook and some colored pencils. While they waited, she drew what looked like ideas for new cookies, their colors popping even from across the table.

Matthew wondered as he watched her slender fingers move across the paper if these were the designs that would make her famous, sitting here in a diner while her brother was in the hospital. Would she talk about that when they interviewed her? Would she mention that one guy Matthew who'd done nothing to help her?

The food came and they both picked at it, an insult to The

Finer Diner's chef.

But when Yvette came over to say hi to Nicolette she didn't say anything, only wrapped Nicolette in a huge hug. She took Nicolette's face in her hands and peered into the younger woman's eyes.

"You look so tired, honey. I'll pack up the rest of your food with some dessert."

Nicolette wiped her eyes. "You don't have to—"

Yvette raised an eyebrow. "Don't even try it, Nic. Let me be a mom."

Yvette glanced over at Nicolette's sketchbook. "Those look awesome!" she beamed. "Austin told me that you were applying to make cookies for Blue Hippo! I loved that movie about the worms in the apple grove."

She reached over and tucked a stray piece of hair behind Nicolette's ear. "Quirky and sweet, just like our Nicolette. You'll be a shoe-in."

Matthew could read the uncertainty behind Nicolette's smile, but she thanked Yvette anyway, and accepted what seemed like twenty bags of food.

Yvette walked them to the door.

"You take care of her, Matthew," she said as a goodbye. Matthew wasn't sure if he was imagining the censure in her gaze, but he just nodded and followed Nicolette out the door.

The silence was magnified in the close confines of his car. Matthew flipped on the radio low, generic pop music creating a low hum.

The food in the back made his car smell like a savory dream, but even then, her sweet smell snuck through, teasing out less than friendly thoughts.

He glanced at her, her head resting against the window and the passing lights throwing her face into dancing patterns of light and dark.

"Do you have a plan if you don't get picked?" he asked, before realizing how that sounded. "For the comic con? Or what if you do get picked? It's pretty soon, right? You'd have to leave."

The girl on the radio was whining about her boyfriend leaving her, and the silence dragged on.

He hazarded a glance at Nicolette to find her giving him a hard stare.

"Why do you care?" she suddenly asked.

"What?" he asked, trying to see her and keep his eyes on the road.

"Why do you care all of a sudden what happens to me, or if I stay or go?"

"It's not—" he started, but she shook her head.

"Of course it's not," she said, a little sadly. "From what I've seen of you these last few days, you care only when you want to. You can't bear to put yourself in an uncomfortable position for other people. You only want to know my plans so that you'll know when you'll finally be rid of me."

"Nicolette, that's not true," he said, trying to keep his own temper in check. For someone who used to idolize him, she sure expected the worst of him. Even if he deserved it.

Nicolette sighed, and seemed to deflate again. "I probably won't apply for the comic con anymore."

"What?" he barked. If he knew one thing about Nicolette Hayes, it was that she wasn't a quitter.

"Seeing Rio today," she said, her voice thick. "It's going to be so much work. Months of rehab, maybe more surgeries. But more than that, Rio's mind..." She sniffled, wiping her face roughly. "He'll have to start all over, without hockey. I think he'll need a lot of help."

She was silent for so long that Matthew hazarded, "Nic?"

"I don't think my dad can do this alone," she confessed. "He needs support too, and there's only me."

They pulled up in front of the house. She was looking right at him. Even in the dim light from the streetlights, she was lit up. Her eyes glittered beneath her glasses, tear tracks stark against her cheeks. She ran her tongue over her bottom lip as her eyes roved over his face, and Matthew took a sharp breath. It seemed like no matter what tension lay between them, Nicolette couldn't stop looking at him.

He couldn't do it anymore. He couldn't pretend that she was like water in his self-made desert. He had to do something about this temptation, and damn the consequences.

He got out of the car and hurried to her side to help her out. He had a speech prepared, pretty words intended to comfort and bolster hope. But with her standing before him, the evening breeze teasing her hair, looking at him with so much tenderness, his mind went blank. And his body took over.

He backed her against the car, loving her small gasp of surprise. Planting his hands on either side of her head, he left enough room for her to escape, shove him aside, and call him an asshole. She didn't budge.

He eased against her. Her soft breasts against his chest felt better than he remembered. He'd left his jacket unbuttoned and standing against her, thigh to thigh, their breaths came in sync, his skin hot and needy under the thin cotton of his T-shirt.

His domination of her was almost complete. Only those sweet lips remained, parted and ready for his taste.

But though she clutched his shoulders, urging him closer, he could still read uncertainty in her eyes.

"Nicolette," he breathed, pressing featherlight kisses across her cheekbones. Her eyelids fluttered shut, and he whispered his next words in her ear. "You're not alone."

Her eyes flew open, and something else burned there. Something that sent his heart rate soaring.

"Matthew," she moaned, and all Matthew's honor died a swift death.

With rough hands, he grabbed her face, capturing her mouth with eager lips. Nicolette opened beneath him, her tongue inviting his to explore. They tangled together in ardent thrusts, her sweet taste making him dizzy and desperate. It was him moaning then, a deep guttural sound he hardly recognized.

She writhed against him, moving her hands beneath his shirt, her small fingers finding his nipples. He grunted as she caressed them with her thumbs, sending a sizzle of pleasure straight to his cock. She smiled against his lips, and he licked that wicked curve.

Not wanting to squander this moment, he rucked up her dress, his own hand finding the curve of her breast. He squeezed her through her bra, the weight a perfect fit in the center of his palm. She arched against him, whispering his name.

Cars were passing, and he could vaguely hear laughter from across the street. But he couldn't stop, wouldn't until she told him to. He could only think that this was a mistake. She was stressed and lonely and looking for some kind of release. Matthew was a convenient body. She couldn't really want him.

But the way she'd said his name, it almost sounded like she did.

He pulled her even closer, wrapping his arms firmly around her. He could feel her heartbeat fluttering against his chest, strong and sure.

He couldn't really be sure of what this was. Everything such a mess between them that even this kiss felt fraught.

All he knew was that when he touched her, he didn't feel so lost.

SEVEN

Nicolette checked the time on her phone. 12:30. Most normal people would be on their lunch break, but Matthew had confessed that he often worked through his lunch breaks. It was such a Matthew thing to do that she only gave him a little grief for it.

Luckily, this seemed to be a rare day where he actually ate. He picked up on the second ring.

"Hey, Nicolette," Matthew's voice greeted her. "What's up?"

He sounded so uncertain that she wanted to roll her eyes. She had hoped they were past all of his keeping her at a distance. She knew Matthew kept things close to the chest. But they'd had their tongues in each other's mouths a dozen times over the last week for crying out loud. A little trust wasn't unwarranted.

She supposed she was partially to blame. This last week had been emotionally draining and completely exhilarating at once. There was so much going on—at the hospital and with her career—and so much unsaid between them, it made sense for him to be a little tentative.

"I have a favor to ask," she said, hoping for a casual tone. "I need you to take me to the airport."

"What?" he asked immediately, his tone growing even more guarded. "Why?"

"One typically goes to the airport to get on an airplane, Matthew," she said, hoping he caught her teasing tone.

A pause. "Are you leaving?" he asked softly.

"Why do you care?" she wondered, the words falling out of her mouth before she could consider them. She'd gone into this call wanting to keep things light, but now that she'd asked, she desperately wanted to know.

"I don't," he muttered. "I mean, I do, but..."

"Smooth," she intoned.

"I just want to know why you're going," he said, starting to sound ticked off.

As if he had a leg to stand on, or even a right to know. Nicolette decided that she was not going to go easy on him.

"Why I'm going?" she asked, pouring on the sugar. If he'd been there in person, he would have seen her sweet, deadly smile. "Well, I just figured that since you didn't want to bother with *us*, I might take off for a while. Get some air. Or do you care?"

She was toying with him now, trying to elicit something from him. It wasn't out of anger. With all that had happened, she'd left her anger behind. There were too many other things to be angry about to direct it at Matthew.

Now all she felt was mounting confusion. Her future was rolling off in directions she had never anticipated. Her brother was still in the hospital, dealing daily with pain and a new reality. Even her father seemed to be a different person, stepping up in ways she'd never expected of him. The only thing Nicolette knew for certain was how she felt about Matthew. She wanted him. Wanted something more than his brief reappearance in her life. But he was so infuriatingly opaque, she had no idea where she stood.

So she did what every self-respecting Hayes kid would do... she messed with him.

She was only headed back to Denver for the weekend. Luz had asked her to help with a big client—a high-profile wedding. She figured she could pack up some more of her things, visit Rhoslyn, and make a few bucks on the side.

Matthew didn't know any of this, of course. She wanted to see what he would do if he thought she would be gone for a while. Maybe all the passion he'd shown her in the past week would dissipate—and maybe it would grow? Clarify? She had hope, small and delicate, that he did care whether or not she stayed. Maybe even enough to fight for her.

It wasn't some outlandish hope. Nicolette had fallen into a routine in the last week. She arrived at the hospital as soon as visiting hours started. She'd try and distract Rio from himself any way she could and stay until they kicked her out. Then she'd head to the diner, where Yvette would stuff her full of food while Austin talked to her in between customers.

And at eight sharp, Matthew would come in and drive her home.

Where they'd climb into the back of his car and kiss until her lips were sore, her panties were drenched, and the ache in her chest was so raw, she thought even screaming Matthew's name wouldn't release it.

It was so strange how natural tangling her legs with his felt. There was no hesitation once they were together in the bubble of the back seat. He mapped her face and neck with his mouth, feeling every part of her he could reach. His big body couldn't move far, and she loved him as her captive. He'd clearly been taking care of himself since quitting hockey, and she relished feeling the hard swell of his bicep or curve of his ass.

Wrapped up in the clandestine nature of their trysts, Matthew revealed another part of himself to her, one she had only seen in flashes. He was warm and funny, his humor wry and self-deprecating. He was also panty-meltingly passionate— he could work her up with just his mouth, leaving her an aching mess by the time he drove away. Most nights, Nicolette would require her own touch to get relief, visions of Matthew sending her over the edge.

She wanted to use this as scientific proof: maybe they weren't fated lovers, but wasn't it worth a shot? Wasn't it enough to want her to stick around?

But for now, she could let that lie. There were other things to worry about, things that could solve all of her problems in one go.

She had a plan. And Matthew was going to be her co-conspirator whether he liked it or not. And she figured since they did their best work in the car, that was where she'd spring this on him.

Matthew still hadn't answered so she forged ahead.

"So can you pick me up after work and take me to the airport?"

"I guess so. Nic, I—"

"Great!" she sang. "See you then."

She dialed Rhoslyn as she finished packing.

"You're coming home?" Rhoslyn squealed, making Nicolette wince.

"Yeah, last minute," Nicolette said, throwing her toiletries in their TSA-sanctioned clear baggie.

"Good, you need a break," Rhoslyn said. "Especially from jerkface Matthew."

Nicolette was quiet for so long that Rhoslyn began to chuckle. "*Is* he still jerkface Matthew?"

"Yes!" she said, the last shred of her pride still hanging on.

"No," she finally admitted. "There may have been kissing, and, um, wandering hands."

"Nic, normally I'd be doing a happy dance for you," Rhoslyn said, and the seriousness of her tone made Nicolette pause in her packing.

"But?" Nicolette said.

"But don't forget the shit this guy said. This was your brother's best friend. You still remember him with rosy memories. But he grew up. So did you. Just...be careful, okay?"

"I am," Nicolette assured, not even believing herself.

Rhoslyn was absolutely right. She was still trying to find the Matthew of her dreams in the man she knew now. She knew he'd changed, and she even liked some of those changes. Adult Matthew was shrewd and sexy, with an edge he'd lacked as a teenager.

But she'd seen glimpses of the boy she'd fallen in love with. He was still in there and though she knew it was dangerous to chase a dream, she found that she couldn't stop. She knew deep inside that they could have something special.

Nicolette was waiting on the porch when Matthew pulled up. Ever the gentleman, he helped her put her suitcase in the back and waited while she buckled herself in. She leaned in and kissed his cheek before settling back in her seat.

He glanced at her, his deep blue eyes dark with worry. This was the first time they'd been in his car with a purpose other than making out like horny teenagers. She almost smiled in triumph when his gaze flicked to her lips before returning to her eyes. Memories of the last week made her shiver. Maybe they had time before he drove her...

"Nic, about before—" Matthew started, his low voice sending shivers down her spine.

"It's okay," she said with a small smile. "I was just being mean. Let's get going, I'll tell you everything on the way."

Still looking a little skeptical, Matthew pulled the car away from the curb. She waited until they were off of residential streets before she started talking.

"I have an idea," she began, her excitement about her plan buoying her. "To help Rio."

She could sense Matthew's hesitation. Of course any mention of Rio would make him clam up. But maybe he would listen to her, now that things between them had changed.

He nodded so she continued.

"He's so depressed, Matthew. He doesn't think there's a point to anything anymore. I am so scared that he might really give up."

It was impossible to convey how dire the situation was with just her words. Matthew hadn't been there. He hadn't seen Rio cry and curse, saying that he was broken. Like so many times in these last interminable weeks, Nicolette began to tear up.

To Matthew's credit, he reached over and squeezed her knee, letting his hand linger there. She covered it with her own before continuing.

"I want to give him something to live for," Nicolette continued. "A reason to work toward getting better."

Matthew nodded for her to continue.

Nic couldn't help the smile that crossed her face. Her plan was perfect and she didn't even know where to start, the words tumbling from her like confetti.

"I want to hold a cookie fundraiser," she explained. "I can't commit to the comic con anymore, there's just no way with Rio's treatment plan. But I'm sure I can put something together to raise the twenty-five thousand dollars I need."

"Twenty-five thousand dollars? For what?" Matthew asked, glancing at her sideways.

This was the big reveal. Nicolette took a deep breath and said, "I want to buy Rio an adaptive hockey sled. I'm going to put it in his room when he moves into the rehab facility. Even if he doesn't want to use it, it will be there as a reminder that what he loved isn't really gone. That nothing we love is really lost."

Matthew had gone as still as one could while still operating a vehicle. His face was completely blank, and Nicolette wondered if he'd heard her. If he understood that she wasn't just talking about Rio healing. That everything that Matthew lost he could have again too—if he wanted to see the possibility.

"That's a terrible fucking idea," Matthew suddenly spat, with so much venom it felt like a slap to the face.

"W-what?" Nicolette sputtered. She couldn't believe that he had said that, that his face was now a picture of anger.

"You're giving up your dreams for your brother," he gritted. "Rio would never do the same for you."

"That's not true," she tried to protest, but Matthew wasn't listening.

"What is it, Nicolette?" he said, jerking to a stop at a red light. "Are you scared? Afraid you wouldn't be accepted to the comic con?"

"No," she said, his betrayal opening a jagged wound on her heart. She'd thought he was on her side. How could he transform so quickly to this angry, mistrustful man? Rhoslyn's warning came echoing back at her. Maybe she didn't really know Matthew after all.

"You need to apply," he went on, driving forward again. "Then you can make a decision with all of the information. There's no reason you couldn't go to Denver for the comic con, then come back to Chicago."

He sounded sure, like the decision was already made. Businessman Matthew, who needed everything to go a certain way. She'd found that driven side of him endearing once. Now it just pissed her off.

"What is wrong with you?" Nicolette yelled, finally finding her voice. "Even if I did get accepted, which I can't rely on, I would have to plan for months in advance. I'd have to design the cookies, make test batches, source ingredients, and hire local help. I would be gone for weeks."

"So that's what you're going to do?" he asked, something nasty in his tone. "Bake a couple cookies, buy a fucking sled, and hang out in your childhood bedroom while everyone dotes on Rio and your career goes down the goddamned toilet? Sounds awesome."

He gave a bitter laugh.

"I don't know why I'm surprised," he went on, vitriol practically dripping from his words. "Everyone always puts Rio first. Rio the fucking demigod. God forbid he actually has to fend for himself like the rest of us plebes."

If he hadn't already removed his hand from her knee, Nicolette would have shoved it away. Hot tears pricked her eyes and she felt achy, like she had the flu. A well of disappointment was threatening to overflow, smothering all the hope she'd had only moments before.

They rode in awful silence, Nicolette's mind whirring like a nest of hornets. It felt like no matter what she did, she pushed Matthew even farther away. He was so stuck up his own ass about whatever had happened, he couldn't see a blossoming future in front of him. He couldn't see that he was the key to so many people's happiness. He wouldn't allow himself his own happiness.

They finally reached the airport, and Nicolette practically shot from the car. Some semblance of chivalry must have been moving Matthew, because he retrieved her suitcase and set it down in front of her. He towered over her, a frown on those beautiful lips.

Angry at herself for even noticing such a stupid thing, she

pulled her suitcase handle up, fully intending to walk away without a word. But a tiny part of her wanted to give him a chance. Despite falling short of her expectations, she wasn't ready to be done with Matthew Collins.

She knew what everyone else failed to see. He had a big heart that had been wounded and he protected it like a scared animal. If she didn't give him the opportunity to prove himself, he might be alone and afraid for the rest of his life. But he was right about one thing. She wasn't going to do the heavy lifting anymore.

Pulling herself up to full height, she met his gaze.

"I don't know what you think my brother did to you," she said, proud of the strength in her voice, "but I'm done trying to fix you. You have zero say over how I help my brother. This is my family and I'll do what I damned well please whether or not you think Rio is worth the sacrifice. As for that"—she shoved her glasses up her nose so she was sure he could not miss her glare—"you clearly have some unfinished business with Rio. I don't get it and I don't want to get involved. This is something you'll have to make better between the two of you. If you're not the complete asshole that you're proving yourself to be, you'll do it before I get back."

"Nicolette—" he tried, but she simply held up a hand.

"That's all I have to say about this, Matthew. Be the man I know you are and fucking fix it." She left Matthew standing on the curb and walked away without looking back. When she finally made it inside the terminal, she sagged against the wall just inside the ticketing area, cursing herself. After all she'd said, all she wanted to do was turn and run back outside and invite him into the safety of the back seat. She wanted to fix everyone, everything. But she knew—she just knew—the only project she could safely commit to was Rio.

But that didn't change the fact that Matthew Collins was

making her crazy. Crazy in lust, in love, and in every other way she could imagine.

Hopefully baking cookies would help.

"HEY, MAN!" Chris Kinsman said, offering a well-calloused hand for Matthew to shake. "Glad we could do this today, I've got all kinds of stuff to show you."

"Great," Matthew said, trying to sound enthusiastic. But no matter what he was doing, Nicolette's challenge haunted him. He hadn't heard from her since she'd left for Denver, and her absence was like a sore muscle he couldn't stretch, the ache low but constant.

He'd practically shouted his agreement when Chris had called wondering if today would work for a site inspection.

"Let's do a walk-through, and then I can show you the plans," Chris suggested, waving Matthew to follow him to the building's dusty stoop.

The building was made of original brick and was shaped like a tall, narrow rectangle. Matthew loved the small details that made it unique.

They stood looking up at it, while Chris explained a little of the building's history.

"It was built as a social club but zoned for mixed use because a church took over and the pastor had a residence on top."

"Sounds a little shady," Matthew joked.

"I've never asked," Chris said, cracking a smile. "I learned that the hard way. Anyway, we're going to remodel so the bottom is a commercial space and keep the top as residential space. You could live above and have your business below."

Matthew nodded and asked Chris to show him inside.

Though it was a bit dated, Matthew could definitely see the potential. Original hardwood floors had been revealed when the carpet was pulled back. The windows were large and gave the space a natural glow. And the residential apartment upstairs was perfect with high ceilings and fixtures that could easily be updated. The clawfoot tub in the bathroom made him wonder if Nicolette liked baths. He could pamper her in such a bath: bubbles, oils, his hands on her slippery skin…

"Do you want to see the plans?" Chris's voice pulled him swiftly from his increasingly dirty thoughts. Nicolette wasn't here. He had to work to do.

They went outside to a worktable, where Chris spread out the plans. He began pointing out the features they planned to include and described what materials they were going to use.

"And I'm planning on making the first level fully ADA accessible," Chris said, pointing to what seemed to be a wheelchair ramp on the plans.

This got Matthew's attention.

"I'm totally down with doing that, but can I ask why?"

Chris's face grew wistful. "My sister Grace has MS," he explained. "She's pretty mobile at this point, but I am always trying to think one hundred steps ahead. I try and make every building I work on better than the county's minimum building specifications. That way, anybody can safely move around my buildings—never a question."

Matthew nodded, his respect for Chis going up by the minute.

"So what about the rest of the building?" Matthew asked, peering at the plans.

"The upper level doesn't really need to be compliant because of planned use. If it's just a renter up there…"

Matthew chewed on his lip, aware that Chris was watching him expectantly.

"What would it take? To make the whole building compliant?"

Chris's grin was bright, like Matthew was speaking his language. "Well, the best way would be to put in an elevator."

Matthew groaned. He'd been afraid of that. Elevators were not exactly cheap and it wasn't like anyone would think worse of him for not installing one. But an idea had sparked to life, standing here in front of all this space, and he couldn't ignore it.

"Give me an estimate on costs," Matthew said, crossing his arms in front of his chest.

Chris stroked his short beard. "With a building this small, pricing will be a little different. The elevator alone will set you back fifty, but I assume you want to, you know, put it in the building."

Matthew chuckled. "No, I was just thinking I'd like to leave it in the backyard."

Chris laughed. "Sounds like an expensive lawn ornament." All seriousness again, he informed Matthew, "We might be able to get away with doing it for seventy-five, but I would budget a hundred just to be safe."

A hundred thousand dollars. Just for a random notion that he wasn't entirely committed to.

"What are you thinking about doing with it?" Chris asked, his curiosity obviously piqued by Matthew's interest in the elevator.

"I thought I might live upstairs and use the first floor for my real estate business," Matthew said. That had been the original plan. Matthew was ready to take the next steps with his business and the building would be a perfect center of operations.

Chris nodded. "I think you're in good shape then. The elevator might be overkill, but you won't hear me talking you out of it. If you ever decide to buy that house in the burbs and rent, you'll have a hell of a lot more options with an elevator. Do you have financing in place to buy?"

"I'm working on it," Matthew said, feeling the excitement that this was becoming real. "It depends on how big of a down payment I'll need to put down."

They talked comps for the next few minutes, about how much Chris thought the building would sell for and what would be a fair price. It felt good to just talk about topics he understood, without any underlying current of emotion. He went a full five minutes without missing Nicolette.

They were wrapping up, and Matthew was about to say goodbye, when Chris asked, "How's Rio Hayes doing?"

It shouldn't have surprised him that Chris would ask, but somehow, he still felt a jolt when he heard Rio's name. What used to be a shot of anger had morphed into something murky that he couldn't quite define, and it had everything to do with Rio's sister.

"As well as could be expected," Matthew said, not sure how to soften the news.

"Shit," Chris whispered, raking a hand through his hair. "Yeah, man. I'm sorry to hear that."

"Yeah," Matthew said, rubbing the back of his hair. He hated the sympathetic look Chris was giving him. He didn't deserve it.

But then Chris's gaze turned contemplative as he studied Matthew.

"Listen, man. I'm gonna give you a little bit of unsolicited advice," he said.

Oh, god, here it comes. The speech about staying strong and everything happened for a reason.

"When my sister was first diagnosed," Chris began, "a lot of people stayed away."

This was not what Matthew had been expecting, and the raw vulnerability on Chris's face made him pay attention.

"They would hear the news and not know what to say to her, or even how to face her. Something like that, it takes everyone's biggest fears and throws them right in their faces."

Chris dropped his eyes to the ground, working his boot into the dirt.

"Some people show up, and they're the ones you want there anyway. But some of the people you want around you the most stay away."

Matthew couldn't help but think of Nicolette, forging ahead despite her fear. Showing up for Rio even when she thought she might lose the things in life that meant the most to her. Her bravery continued to astound him, especially in light of what Chris was telling him.

Chris sighed and lifted his head. "They're not good or bad, those people. Something like that, it brings up a lot of shit. Old fears and hurts. People just have to process things in their own way. I may be overstepping my bounds," Chris continued. "And I know this is cheesy as fuck, but I had to learn it the hard way. Every moment is a gift and all we have is the moment. I know Rio must be hurting like hell right now, and the last thing he'll want to see is his strong, successful friend stroll in on two perfect legs. But just keep showing up. No matter how tough it gets, that's what true friends do."

Matthew nodded, because he wasn't sure what else to do. Chris was absolutely right and completely wrong. He and Rio weren't "true friends." It wasn't about facing his fears or even not wanting to upset anyone. It was about the one person who was supposed to have Matthew's back stabbing him in it and living a carefree life of ease and accolades.

He was so tired of having to be righteous, of having everyone tell him that he was in the wrong. Yes, Rio had received life-changing injuries. But that would not absolve him of the wounds Matthew had sustained, his life altered forever. Wounds no one could see. And so no one cared.

How could he show up for Rio when he couldn't forgive him?

"Thanks, Chris," Matthew said, because the other man meant well. He'd obviously known pain and it couldn't have been easy for him to share that with Matthew.

Chris smacked Matthew hard on the back. "Anytime, man. You'll be okay."

He would. Matthew had absolute faith in his ability to survive. He wondered what the costs of his survival were.

Leaving the building site, he wasn't sure what to do with himself. Austin was working tonight, and Keith was probably resting at home. Austin had told Matthew that Keith had had to go back to working part time and was catching up on sleep whenever he could.

Which meant Rio was alone at the hospital right now. Despite Nicolette's ultimatum, Matthew hadn't even thought about going to see Rio. Reaching his car, he pulled up directions to the hospital. He remembered what Chris had told him.

Maybe he would go. Maybe he would show up.

Once he got behind the wheel, Nicolette's angry words from the airport floated back to him. He wondered what she would do if he didn't visit Rio by the time she came back. Drag him kicking and screaming to the hospital, where Rio would just laugh him right back out the door? Never speak to him again? The thought of never kissing Nic in the back of his car again gave him pause.

And that was the kicker. Nic. All roads led back to her faith in him. To the man she believed him to be. The bullshit of it all was that she had no idea what kind of a man her own brother was. What he'd done to ruin Matthew and end his dreams before they even began. He wondered what she expected if he *did* visit Rio? A tearful reunion, some apologies maybe, and then Matthew + Rio = BFF? In some ways he suspected that Nicolette still saw him and her brother through her childish lens: they might argue or even not talk for a while, but eventually all fences would be mended. She had no fucking idea.

There was so much she didn't know about her own brother. If she knew, would it make a difference?

Or would she choose Rio anyway? She'd have to, wouldn't she? The thought that he could lose Nic over the rift between him and Rio gave Matthew pause.

The hospital could wait. Something tugged him to turn around, and soon he was driving slowly up the Hayes's street.

He drifted to a stop in front of the house. Keith Hayes was sitting on the porch swing, a tumbler of scotch held loosely in his hand. He was staring off into space, looking deep in thought rather than vacant, a relief to Matthew.

At the sound of Matthew locking his car, Keith snapped to attention, a huge smile growing on his face.

Matthew climbed the porch steps with his hands in his pockets.

"Can I join you, Keith?"

Keith patted the seat next to him. "I've been hoping you'd stop by. I've been wanting to talk to you. Scotch?"

Matthew fetched his own glass, and Keith poured him a healthy portion.

"I see you remembered where I hid the good stuff," Keith teased, watching Matthew take a sip like a proud father.

Matthew laughed. "I would apologize but I needed it."

"Then no apology needed," Keith said, still smiling that warm smile.

Matthew ducked his head, unable to handle the affection.

This man was the only father he'd ever had and had no reason to be treating Matthew like he was a deserving son.

Keith seemed to sense the change in Matthew. He stared down at the glass in his hands, and he looked so tired Matthew almost told him to go to bed.

"I feel like I owe you an apology. I always wanted to tell you how sorry I was about what happened with your parents," Keith said.

That was not what Matthew had been expecting to hear, but Keith pushed on, like he'd been thinking about this for a long time.

"You stopped coming around after that. I just thought you were embarrassed. I thought maybe you would deal with it in your own time or ask for help when you needed it. I never thought a decade would go by and we wouldn't see you. I'm... I'm sorry I didn't reach out myself."

"Please, you don't need to apologize," Matthew protested, horrified. "It was my fault. I didn't even come to Robin's memorial and—"

Keith waved a dismissive hand in the air. "Son, you were living your own life. Rio was in Italy, and I hardly expected you to come cry with Robin's friends around the urn. Still, I think Nicolette would have liked to see you."

Matthew couldn't tell if Keith was implying something, but he thought it best to steer the conversation away from Nicolette. There was something more pressing he wanted to ask.

"What did you mean, about my parents?" Mathew asked carefully. He supposed their legal troubles had been no big secret, but some insidious curiosity made him want to know what Keith thought.

"Oh, you know, that you lost your scholarship."

Matthew reared back as if Keith had spit in his face. He

might as well have. He said it so matter-of-factly, a sad fact but the loss dulled by time.

He couldn't believe that Keith, the man he loved as a father, could sit there and casually mention his scholarship, the scholarship that Rio had cost him by ratting out his parents. The reason that Keith hadn't seen Matthew was that Rio had cost him everything. Another piece of collateral damage.

A thousand words sat on the tip of Matthew's tongue, but none came out. He just wasn't ready to reopen that wound. He wondered if he ever would be.

"Do you talk to your parents much?" Keith asked, filling the awkward silence that had fallen.

"Not if I can help it," Matthew answered woodenly.

"Why?" Keith asked, looking genuinely curious.

His apparent care made Matthew even more unhappy, but he chose his next words with intent. "When someone shows me how little they care for me or that they will put themselves first even if it hurts me...I've been betrayed by too many people, I guess. Not worth putting in the effort with them."

Keith shook his head. "That's a pretty sad way to see the world, son. Maybe the people you love the most are just human. Maybe it's not really about you, but about them." He paused for a moment, considering his words. "What you have to ask yourself is if their motivations are truly selfish, or if they just, you know..."

"Fucked up?" Matthew supplied, unable to stop his grin.

Keith chuckled. "Yeah. Maybe they just made dumb mistakes, and some very innocent people got caught in the middle."

Matthew's smile drained from his face. Of course it would seem like that to Keith. His beloved son had just fucked up, no big deal. It all fell on Matthew to forgive. Forgive Rio, forgive his parents. It was all the same. Somehow, the responsibility rested heavy on *his* shoulders.

He took a long sip of scotch, the warm burn of alcohol easing his tight shoulders. He looked Keith straight in the eyes and laid his challenge out.

"What if those fucked-up but well-intentioned people never apologize in the first place?"

Keith looked at Matthew as if he was a little simple. "Son, if you never talk to them again, how would they ever get the chance?"

EIGHT

If Nicolette never had to wait in a baggage claim again, it would be too soon. People jostling for their bags, bumping their sharp edges into her shins. Kids screaming and running just out of their parents' reach. She'd always thought this would be a place of relief, the end of a long journey.

She watched a small dog take a piss on someone's suitcase.

Nope.

Turning her focus back to her small mountain of luggage, she did some mental calculations. Three more bags. She'd packed up a bunch of stuff and had put the rest in storage. She could sort it all out later. For now, she was home.

Good thing that Dad had agreed to pick her up and bring the truck. She might have gone a little overboard with her packing.

Her magenta and green suitcase came rattling around the corner. Once again it was tangled with the bag next to it. Nicolette sighed and prepared to do battle, when a rather well-shaped arm reached passed her and plucked the bag from the belt.

Another sigh passed her lips. That arm definitely did not belong to her dad. She pushed her glasses up her nose and prepared for another kind of battle. Turning, she saw Captain Jerkface himself, holding her suitcase and looking very pleased with himself. A world of difference from the last expression she'd seen on his face. Her heart managed to sink and flutter at the same time.

"You're not my dad," she accused. "Who begged you to come get me this time?"

"No one," Matthew said, his toothy grin growing wider. "I asked Keith when you were getting in and offered to pick you up."

Damn it, he looked so good, like she could lick him to reach the surprise center. But she would not relent so easily, no matter his newly discovered gallantry.

"I wanted my dad to get me," she said with obvious vinegar. "He has a truck and I have all this." She waved to the embarrassingly large pile of bags as if he was so dense he might have missed it.

But his smile was unwavering. "Your dad loaned me the truck. He's taking the day off. Said he's gonna work on his golf swing."

A tiny smile twitched to life on Nicolette's face, but she smothered it quickly.

"I don't—" she started, but he began walking away.

"Wait here, I'll get a luggage cart," he called.

After finagling all of her bags onto a cart and into the truck, Nicolette finally put him on the spot, demanding the one thing she wanted to know.

"I hope you being here means that you've seen Rio."

He maneuvered the car through the airport traffic, staring straight ahead.

"Nope," he said. "I'm here for you."

"Matthew, that's not—" she began, ready to rip him a new one, but she didn't seem able to get a word in edgewise today.

"I was thinking about your cookie fundraiser idea," he said, which immediately got her attention. Besides Matthew and her family, it was the thing most heavy on her mind. "I don't think you've thought this through," he continued. She gritted her teeth at his assumption but let him continue. Matthew was a businessman. He might have a good idea or two.

"I ran some numbers, and to even get close to your goal, let alone break even, you'd have to bake an insane number of cookies. Like, thousands. And where would you bake all those cookies? You'd need a license in Cook County. You'd need a commercial kitchen. You have no help and no capital."

Nicolette's heart deflated. She had known it would be a ton of work. But when he put all the details in front of her...of course she hadn't worked all of that out yet.

"And if you want the sled...Nic, I just don't think this is the best way to do this."

She wanted to yell at him, demand why he always seemed to be the object of her disappointment when all she wanted was the simple joy of liking him and the comfort of helping her brother.

But he wasn't done. "And I still think you're killing your own career before it starts. Your dreams deserve attention just as much as Rio."

He threw a tender smile at her. "You're so damned talented, Nicolette, and you have a chance to do what you want. Or try something new. Or anything."

He seemed on a roll now, a tinge of excitement in his words. "What if you *did* get the comic con? You would just come back after. You said yourself Rio's recovery could take years. Are you really going to wait for Rio to sort out his life to become star of your own?"

Overwhelmed by his litany of truths, Nicolette let her anger have free rein.

"What the fuck, Matthew? This is your idea of a homecoming? You haven't seen Rio and you pick me up at the airport so you can shoot my dreams in the face on top of making me feel like a grade-A moron? Fuck you!"

She sucked in a breath, desperate to hear what he had to say for himself.

"You're not a moron," Matthew said calmly, as if she hadn't just exploded an emotion bomb all over him. "Your ideas are a little weird, but all you need is a little help. Some support."

"What are you talking about?" she said, exasperated. "And where are you going?"

In her bluster, she hadn't noticed that Matthew had taken the wrong exit for her house. They were now on an unfamiliar street, and Matthew made no move to right his course.

"Will you just let me show you something?" he asked, so earnest that she calmed slightly. "After you see it, you can decide what you want to do."

Nicolette considered. There was no real harm in humoring him. She could always do what she'd been planning, with or without his help.

"Okay," she relented, and he seemed to sigh in relief.

A few minutes later, Matthew navigated the truck into the parking garage of an upscale condo complex.

Matthew ran around to her side of the car before she could get out. He offered her his hand, his eyes so warm she found it hard to breathe.

"Come on," he said.

For a moment Nicolette wondered if he was offering more than just his hand. Pushing down those ridiculously girlish thoughts, she let him help her from the car.

But he didn't let go of her hand.

He led her out of the garage and around the back of the complex. A large hexagonal building sat there, painted mint green and posh as all get out.

Finally dropping her hand, Matthew shuffled through his keys, and let them in.

Nicolette goggled for a moment at the room in front of her. Following the same hexagonal shape, five delicate pillars separated the space into different areas. Leather couches sat snug near a fireplace in one, a case of books and games within easy reach. A bar dominated another area, just waiting to be filled with liquor. A pool table was another feature. The other two areas and the middle of the room sat empty and full of possibility, and a pool glittered just beyond a pair of French doors.

It was gorgeous. The warm honey-colored wood floors and cream walls leant the place a sophisticated air, while feeling cozy at the same time.

Nicolette wandered farther in, looking around in awe.

"This is amazing," she breathed. A glance at Matthew showed him looking pleased with himself. "What is this?"

He joined her in the middle of the room, bringing his warm scent with him. She had to focus very hard on the pattern in the granite of the bar to hear what he was saying.

"This is the clubhouse for this complex. I live here."

Nicolette glanced up in surprise. Even if she hadn't seen the condos coming in, the clubhouse alone would have told her: this place was not cheap.

She didn't know why it surprised her that Matthew had made it. He'd always been a hard worker with a perfectionist edge. But he'd also always been that perpetually hungry boy who never seemed to have enough. She'd known even as a child that Matthew spent so much time at their house not just for the company, but out of necessity.

"I love it," Nicolette said, wanting him to know that she loved his success. "But what's this got to do with cookies?"

Another secret smile, and he beckoned her to a door just behind the bar. Behind it, shining like some hazy dream, was a commercial kitchen.

Nicolette wandered in, drawn like a magnet, running her hands across the stainless-steel counters. Whoever had stocked this kitchen had a baker's heart. There was a mixer, a dough hook hanging along with the other attachments. There were rolling racks to place cooling trays of food on. And, be still her beating heart, there was even a proofing oven, where dough could live while it was rising.

She wandered to the convection oven in a daze, peeking inside. It was immaculate. She thought she might swoon. Instead she put on her best nonchalant face and straightened.

"This is a good oven," she announced to Matthew. "I think I could work with this."

Matthew's joyful laugh rang off of the metal surfaces and stroked across her skin, raising the hair on her arms. He leaned against the counter, limbs long and relaxed. She wished she had a camera to capture the moment. *Hottie Heating Up the Kitchen.* They'd give her prime gallery space.

"I think you should brush off your portfolio and apply for the con. Don't let your talent go to waste, Nic. You can always decide what to do when the time comes. But if you never even try..." He spread his hands. "I think you'll regret it."

Her relaxed feeling faded. He was still on about this. Damn it, he made it all sound so easy, dangling the hopes she'd been trying to set aside temptingly in her face.

She crossed her arms, hating that she always had to put this barrier between them.

"Why do you care so much?" she demanded. "Why would you even want to help me?" She glanced around the kitchen wistfully. "And what about this space? It can't be cheap to rent out."

"It's not," he agreed, remaining infuriatingly calm in the face of her suspicion. "But I asked the association if they would work with me on a rate and they agreed. I can't guarantee it will be a *good* rate, but we'll work something out."

"Okay..." she said, trying not to get tongue-tied over the fact that he'd definitely done some thinking, and planning, and scheming while she was away. He might not have fixed what she'd asked him to, but he'd certainly fixated on...her. "You didn't answer my question," Nicolette said, unwilling to let him wiggle out of this. "Why are you so eager to help?"

Pushing himself off of the counter, he came to stand in front of her. With gentle fingers he pushed a lock of her hair behind her ear. He brought his hand to rest on her shoulder, the heat of his palm permeating her shirt.

"Because," he said, his voice soft like he was confessing. "When I needed help the most, no one was there to pick me up."

"What do you mean?" she whispered, watching his eyes grow dark.

"It's not important," he said, and before she could argue that *yes, it fucking was*, he continued. "What is important is that you are amazing, and you deserve a chance."

With that, he walked past her back out to the main room.

Nicolette stared at the swinging door, unable to fight the tenderness she felt for this man. Yes, he was weirdly cagey. Yes, he was stubborn and stoic and generally aggravating.

But ever since he'd come back into her life, all that he'd done had been for her. When all eyes were understandably on Rio, Matthew was always looking at her.

He was kind. And surprisingly funny. And so sexy she'd gotten off countless times imagining his hands on her.

Nicolette shoved through the door, only to be brought up short. Matthew was just on the other side. He'd been waiting for her. They reached for each other at the same time, Nicolette practically launching herself into his arms. Matthew staggered backward and hit one of the pillars, then spun her around so it was her back against it.

She wriggled against him, trying to get as close as possible, and whined when he chuckled against her mouth.

"Slowly," he whispered, before licking the corner of her mouth.

"No," she burst, and pulled his face to hers.

His mouth opened in surprise and she took the opportunity, sliding her tongue against his. He moaned low in his throat, and met her tongue again, more forcefully this time.

It seemed all of his cute plans to go slow were abandoned. His kisses grew urgent and a little sloppy as he tasted every inch of her mouth. He grabbed a handful of her ass with one hand, while the other struggled with the buttons on her shirt.

Nicolette on the other hand seemed only able to grab onto his hard biceps and hold on for dear life. His touch was addictive, trailing pleasure across her skin like a brush fire. She thought she could just kiss him forever, his talented tongue enough to sustain her.

And then he slid one of those shapely thighs between hers, nudging her legs apart. He pushed his hips against hers, his straining cock rubbing against her core.

Nicolette saw stars. Breaking the kiss, she threw her head back as he moved against her again.

"Oh, shit," she whispered to the ceiling, as Matthew dragged his teeth down the column of her throat.

Matthew Collins was a sex god. Who knew?

She knew. She knew she needed more. She needed all of him.

With shaking hands, she started to fumble with the button of his jeans. A gentle hand on her wrist stopped her.

"Nicolette," he said, his voice low and husky.

He was looking at her a little regretfully, and Nicolette's stomach bottomed out.

He didn't want her. This was a mistake. He couldn't sleep with his friend's sister for fuck's sake—

"I don't have a condom," he said, and she saw that what she'd read as regret was sheepishness.

"But I have some in my condo," he rushed on. "If that's what you—"

"Why didn't you take me there in the first place?" she demanded.

"Well, I didn't know that we—"

"Oh, come on!" she said, grabbing his hand and pulling him to the door.

Halfway down the path, Nicolette realized her shirt was flapping in the breeze, her polka-dot bra on display for everyone's viewing pleasure. She also had no idea where Matthew's condo was.

She laughed, tugging him faster.

She didn't care where they were going. All she cared about was that Matthew's hand was in hers, that he wanted her. Suddenly her choices seemed endless, a myriad of possibilities spilling ahead of her like a batch of unicorn macaroons.

As silly as it seemed, even to her, she didn't feel scared anymore.

THEY STUMBLED INTO HIS CONDO, Matthew barely managing to close the door behind them. For a few sweet moments, they stood in the entranceway in each other's arms, rapid breaths syncing. He stared down into her flushed face and felt a sharp tug deep in his chest. She was so beautiful, so alive and real and everything he'd ever needed. He didn't know what he'd done to deserve this.

So he kissed her, slow and deep, like he could never get enough. She gave a breathy moan and dug her fingers into his hair. Her nails scored his scalp, the pleasurable sting like a dart straight to his dick.

She still felt miles away, not nearly close enough. Without breaking their kiss, he lifted her in his arms, her legs wrapping automatically around his hips. The fit was perfect. She was perfect.

He was reluctant to take his mouth from hers, but there were so many delectable parts of her and he meant to taste them all. Moving his legs and trailing kisses across her jaw was difficult—especially with a soft woman pressed against his raging hard-on—but he was determined to do this right.

"Where are we going?" she gasped as he licked the shell of her ear.

"Bathroom," he grunted, toeing the door of said room open.

"Wha..." she managed as he began rummaging around in a drawer, holding her up with one arm.

"Condom," he explained, holding up the foil package.

Something flickered in her gaze, and it weakened his knees when he recognized what it was. Desire. Not that he'd doubted her. But that one look told him the thing his thirsty heart yearned for— she didn't just want him for his body. She wanted *him*.

But he still had to be sure.

"You want this?" he asked softly, resting his forehead against hers.

She nipped his bottom lip playfully. "Always the responsible Matthew," she teased, moving her hips against his aching cock until he gasped. "What is Matthew like when he has fun?" she continued, tapping her chin innocently.

He growled with dramatic menace, roughly reclaiming her mouth. He could feel every inch of her pressed against him, her nipples sharp points against his chest. He was so worked up he didn't know if he could make it to the bedroom, ready to take her against the bathroom counter.

No. While they could explore the possibilities of sex in the bathroom next time, right now he wanted something different.

The thought sent up a flare of fear, momentarily outshining his lust.

What did he want, exactly?

He wanted more than a fast fuck. He wanted to connect to her, to share some of that light she carried, that pure joy.

He wanted to let her in.

Matthew Collins didn't let people in. That was rule number one.

But for Nicolette Hayes, he would break all the rules.

With confident steps, he carried Nicolette to his bedroom.

Where he promptly stumbled on the area rug, landing hard on his knees to protect Nicolette. He teetered forward, and she ended up on her back, with him nestled between her legs.

"Damn it," he breathed, his face flaming. He felt like a bumbling teenager again, always trying to keep up with the big boys.

He started to pull away, but Nicolette grabbed the front of his shirt.

"Where do you think you're going?" she said, running a foot down the back of his leg. Somehow with just her wicked smile, his insecurities melted away, replaced by the buzz of anticipation.

He started unbuttoning the rest of her already mostly

undone top. "Nicolette, there's a perfectly good bed two feet away."

She sat up and tossed her top over her shoulder. Lying back down, she wiggled like she was getting comfortable. "I like it here."

He laughed and pressed a lingering kiss between her breasts. He could feel her pulse tick up, and he resigned himself. If she wanted to fuck on the floor, they would fuck on the floor.

"At least let me get a blanket," he said. He could just reach the bed and pulled his comforter off. He made her roll on her side so he could tuck it fully under her. He took the opportunity to take off his clothes.

He was aware of her eyes hot on him as he finally stepped out of his boxer briefs, his erection jutting up like a flagpole.

"Matthew," she whispered, sitting up on her arms as if to get a closer look. "Jesus, you're gorgeous."

The words made him grow harder, even as he couldn't meet her gaze. He'd never been particularly shy with his body, but that was because he never really thought about it. It was just a mass of muscle and skin to get him from point A to point B.

With Nicolette, he felt truly naked. And he was okay with that.

Dropping to his knees, he divested her of her jeans and flats. He watched with rapt attention as she removed her bra, and God, he felt like he'd won a gold medal.

She was so beautiful it hurt. Her breasts were perfect, because they belonged to her. Full teardrops of smooth skin, her nipples were tight and waiting for his touch.

He wanted to go slow, to treat her like she mattered to him. But as he reached for her his self-control crumbled. Pulling to her to him, he dug desperate fingers into her back and took one breast in his mouth, swiping her nipple roughly with his tongue.

He was vaguely aware of her tossing her head back, his name an oath on her lips. He moved his attention to her other breast. She ran her nails down his back, urging him on. He teased her with his lips and teeth, until her moans grew high and pleading.

Not to be outdone, Nicolette reached between them to caress his cock. Her cool fingers felt like heaven on his scorching skin. She was more delicate than him, her feather-light strokes driving him to distraction. If he didn't stop her soon, this was going to be over fast.

Lifting his head reluctantly, he grabbed her wrist, stopping her ministrations.

"Lie back," he ordered, his voice hoarse with need.

She settled back against the blanket, letting her legs fall open. Matthew hooked the sides of her panties and pulled them off.

"Fuck," he swore. She was the prettiest thing he'd ever seen, all wet and ready. Ready for him.

He did the only thing he could. Leaning over, he pressed a kiss to her sweet center. Pulling her thighs farther apart, he began lavishing her clit with his tongue, feeling like a god when she arched against him.

Needing more of her, he slid a finger into her tight heat, followed by a second.

"Oh, fuck, *Matthew!*" she cried, threading her fingers in his hair. She pushed him closer and he let his eyes flutter closed, her pleasure like a drug.

He knew she was close by her breathing and the tremble in the thigh he was clutching. With one last kiss, he pulled back, taking his hand with him.

After a moment, Nicolette cracked one eye, looking at him with censure.

"Really?" she huffed. "You're gonna play that way?"

He almost laughed at her indignation. Instead he reached for the condom.

She watched with parted lips as he tore the packet open and rolled it down his length. Settling himself fully between her legs, he kissed the hollow of her throat, her chin, the corner of her mouth.

"Yes. The first time you come, it's going to be around my cock."

Nicolette licked her lips. "Dirty boy. Who knew?"

"You did," he said, reaching between them to line himself up with her entrance. Her breath hitched and he smiled down at her. "You were always the one who saw me."

"Matthew—" she tried, but he silenced her with a quick thrust of his hip, seating himself fully inside of her.

"Oh, God," she moaned, spreading herself wider. She dug her heels into his ass as he started a rhythm. He abandoned the notion of a sweet "first time." Right now, he just needed to feel her, to give her everything she deserved.

As his hips took over, he watched her take him, her head thrown back in erotic bliss. Her breasts were bouncing with the force of his movement, her knees pulled high. The soft sighs escaping her lips threaded through his veins like whiskey. The sight made him push harder.

He'd never felt this turned on. It was awesome.

And terrifying.

Because suddenly he could see their connection was so much more potent than the points between their bodies. They had history and shared memories. She understood where he came from and how hard he'd worked to get to this moment.

But more important than the past was that Nicolette was

possibility. All her goodness and stubbornness. All of her quirks and her huge heart. She would stand by him despite his foibles. They could grow together.

Matthew felt too big for his skin and had to rest his head against Nicolette's collarbone. He inhaled deep, that ridiculously sweet scent making him grin like an idiot.

This was right. This was how it was supposed to be. He'd been searching for a home for so long, and it had been her all along.

"Matthew!" Nicolette suddenly cried. "I—"

"I've got you, sweetheart," he said. He angled his thrusts higher. Murmuring endearments in her ear, he felt her muscles clamp around him, and he drank her cries with kisses as she came.

Her bliss was enough to get Matthew off. He followed her seconds later, groaning embarrassingly loud as he came hard, spilling violently into the condom.

Completely boneless, he sprawled atop her for what seemed like ages. Their breathing slowed, but their heartbeats were in sync. Matthew had never felt so tension-free. He wondered if he would simply melt away and evaporate into a very satisfied mist.

"Matthew," Nicolette said softly. "I do love your muscles, but they're very heavy."

Laughing, he rolled off of her and gathered her close. He stroked her face and hair, unable to stop touching her.

"That was..." she said, bracing a hand on his chest.

"I know," he said.

"I've never..." she said again.

"I know," he answered, trying to conceal the enormous grin that was threatening to take over his face.

Suddenly a look of complete panic crossed her face, and Matthew's body tightened in alarmed anticipation.

"Shit, my dad," she said. "He was expecting me hours ago. He's probably freaking out."

"Damn it," Matthew said, sitting up. "I gotta get you back. He's probably more worried about his truck, though."

Nicolette smacked his arm playfully but got up and started gathering her clothes. Matthew watched her with undisguised appreciation, wondering how long he could keep her before her dad would really notice.

"What should we tell him?" Nicolette asked, pulling her panties on.

Matthew got distracted watching her breasts disappear into her bra.

"Tell him that we toured the kitchen," he said, hating how her jeans got to be against her legs. "You decided to follow your original plans, and I talked you out of the sled idea."

The temperature in the room dropped. Nicolette had completely frozen, her shirt clutched in her hand. Her eyes glittered with anger and her breath caught in her throat.

"Damn," she said bitterly. "I think I finally get it. This is why you and Rio fell out, isn't it?" She started buttoning her shirt with shaking fingers. "You never listen to what anyone else wants. You just steamroll ahead, your needs always coming first."

"Nic—" he tried, but she went on.

"Don't you understand?" she cried, sliding her feet into her flats. "I *want* to do this for Rio! He's my brother for fuck's sake!"

She stormed from the room. Matthew saved a little of his dignity and pulled on his boxer briefs and shirt before following. Her accusations were such a departure from what they'd done that he wasn't sure what he was feeling. He only knew he had to make this right.

But as soon as he got to the living room, she rounded on

him again.

"Where were you for the last decade, anyway?" she accused. "You don't know how much he missed you. How much your abandonment broke his heart. I was *there*, Matthew. I know."

And there it was. As always, it was all about Rio. It was always about someone else, and Matthew just got thrown under the bus. He could tell she wasn't done, so he crossed his arms. Let her rail. Let her blame him. He knew how to shut it all out.

"I know Rio can be difficult sometimes," she conceded, softening a little. "He's full of himself and he can be so dense. But you and Rio and Austin were brothers! They are your truest friends! But now I see why they stopped talking to you." She shook her head, throat working with some emotion. "I never knew you were like this. I worshipped you because I thought you were *it*. You held everyone together. You were the loyal one."

Something deep in Matthew snapped. This woman who had wormed her way into his heart was talking about things she had no idea about. He was supposed to be the one she protected now, or at least trusted. Within five minutes of the most intense connection of his life, she'd turned on him. He just couldn't get it right. But he also didn't have to sit back and take it anymore.

"Loyal?" he laughed. "Why don't you go ask your brother about loyalty? Just give him a call in the hospital and ask him who really cost me my scholarship and hockey career. You might learn something really interesting. I just don't want to see him ruin your life like he ruined mine!"

Nicolette stared at him like she was staring at a stranger. That cut deeper than anything she'd said. Whatever they'd had was now severed.

"You're an asshole," she spat.

"Well, we can't all be teenage daydreams," he cut back, hating himself more with each word.

She held out her hand. "Give me the keys to Dad's truck."

He found them lying by the door, where he'd tossed them in his haste to get in Nicolette's pants. What an idiot he was.

He pressed the keys into her palm, careful not to make contact with her skin.

Without any preamble, she strode to the door and swung it open.

"I don't want to see you again. Ever," she said without turning around. And then she was gone, leaving the door swinging on its hinges.

Matthew padded over to the door and closed it gently. He felt fragile, like even a gust of wind would shatter him.

He wandered to his room and gathered up the comforter, shoving it into the washing machine. He couldn't bear having her scent drifting through his condo.

Easing himself down on the couch, he contemplated drinking himself into oblivion. But it wasn't worth the hangover. He was in enough pain as it was.

For the first time in his life, Matthew had thought he'd found something real. Something good. He should have known that he couldn't trust that something so wonderful would be his.

Good thing he was used to dealing with heartbreak. He knew exactly what to do. Tomorrow he'd get up bright and early and head to work. He'd throw himself back into his job and live how he had before Nicolette Hayes had barged back into his life. Busy and alone.

But that was for tomorrow. Tonight he'd sit here, head in his hands, and dream about the impossible woman who was never his to begin with.

NINE

The clock above the oven read quarter to six. Nicolette had been here for an hour already, arriving at the diner when it was still dark. She hadn't been able to sleep and had texted Yvette the night before to ask if she could use her oven. Yvette offered to pick her up on her way in. She could work before opening to stay out of the way of the cooks.

Now, she and Yvette worked in companionable silence. Yvette was prepping vegetables for the line, and Nicolette was preparing dough. She hadn't decided what these cookies would become, but she found comfort in the exactness of baking. Put a certain number of ingredients in, get a certain result.

Not so with people. She could do all the right things and still end up with a complete mess.

Nicolette decided to mix the ingredients the old-fashioned way, her arm aching a little as she beat the sticky mess of dough.

She caught Yvette throwing her concerned looks and Nicolette couldn't blame her. Nicolette's reflection in the mirror that morning had revealed a pale face with exhausted eyes. She looked like she'd been through the ringer.

The dough had reached the right consistency. Sprinkling flour on the counter, Nicolette began rolling it out, smoothing all the wrinkles and bubbles.

Last night, she'd gone straight to her room, throwing some excuse to her dad, who'd known better than to follow. The tiny room trapped her in, put her in close confines with her rage and too many memories.

How dare he? she'd thought. He'd lulled her into believing in him. With him, she'd felt a deep want being filled. Nicolette had set her bottle adrift with a coded message. She'd thought that he'd not only fished it from the ocean, but that he'd understood her cryptic words. Everyone always called her quirky and cute, but Matthew was the first to see her under all that.

And then he'd thrown it all back in her face, revealing himself to be selfish and a little cruel. He'd tried to twist her words to deflect the blame. But worse, he'd mocked her feelings, reducing her long-held feelings for him to a silly girlish crush.

Pacing her room, Nicolette began tearing pictures off the wall, tossing them carelessly in the garbage. The violence of the act gave her a thrill, fueling her anger as she replayed his words.

He thought the past didn't matter? That Rio had ruined his life? Fine. She would move the hell on. She'd remove herself from his life. God forbid she remind him of his inability to let go. She could face her future without him.

That thought had snagged hold of her racing indignation, making her pause. She glanced down at the picture in her hand. It was the one of the Terrible Trio all holding Nicolette mermaid style.

She'd never really noticed before, but while everyone was mugging for the camera, Matthew was looking at Rio, like her brother had just spoken and distracted him.

Rio was like that, though. Every eye in the room always fixed on him, and he outshone everyone around him.

Like a deflated balloon, Nicolette sank onto her bed, cradling the picture in her hands. A quiet boy like Matthew would have always been in Rio's shadow. No matter the strength of their friendship, she realized, Matthew would have always been a step behind.

Everything Matthew had said came back to her and she studied every word like a detective. All his veiled hints and his refusal to see Rio fell together and this picture was a clue.

Nicolette suddenly felt cold. What if she'd been wrong? Her own faith in her family could have blinded her to the truth: that Rio was the villain and Matthew the innocent victim.

She'd taken a shower, trying to rinse Matthew from her skin, and lain awake in her pillow cocoon for hours. She didn't know whom to believe. No matter who was really at fault, a man she loved had done something awful.

Now she stood in The Finer Diner's kitchen, sifting through her cookie cutters. But nothing spoke to her. All she heard were the echoes of Matthew's passion—and his rage.

If Matthew was telling the truth, maybe he was right about everything. Maybe the fundraiser was a pipe dream, and she needed to make comic con her priority. Or maybe she should forget about everything and just get a job. Someone in Chicago was bound to need a baker. Maybe Mora had some connections, that or one of the other hockey wives.

The thought was depressing and made her even more confused. Because what if she was putting Rio before her own needs? Working in someone else's kitchen was not her goal. She wanted her own business and the room to stretch her creative wings. She needed friends, a plan...a sled. God, the list of reasons why she felt like shit grew longer the more she thought about it.

"Ready for breakfast, honey?"

Yvette's voice snapped Nicolette out of her stupor. The older woman was standing there holding two plates piled high with eggs, potatoes, and bacon. Nicolette's stomach grumbled in response and Yvette chuckled.

"Here, take these to a booth. I'll bring some coffee."

Nicolette chose a booth by the window, and watched the rising sun paint the Chicago sky with streaks of pink and orange.

Yvette settled across from her, pushing a steaming cup of coffee in her direction.

Nicolette drank deeply, her eyes fluttering shut. It was amazing how something so simple could feel so good. Like Matthew's hands.

Her eyes shot open, and she found Yvette staring at her expectantly.

"You gonna tell me what's going on," she asked dryly, "or am I gonna have to hold your breakfast hostage?"

Nicolette took a defiant bite of eggs, but Yvette wouldn't be moved.

Nicolette sighed. "I'm just confused," she confessed. "I want to do a fundraiser for Rio's sled, but I'm not sure enough people would contribute. I even thought I might start a non-profit to support sled hockey in Chicago, but..."

"But?" Yvette prompted.

"Someone told me..." she started, then cleared her throat, taking a different tack. "What if Rio really doesn't want anything to do with hockey anymore? I thought it might be inspiring, but what if it's just painful?"

A horrible thought occurred to her. What if this sled thing wasn't about Rio at all, but about her? She wanted so badly to fix everything, and she hadn't really considered what her brother might want. Was it possible that she was as selfish as she'd accused Matthew of being?

It was a possibility she had to consider. But she was sure she was doing this because she loved Rio. At the end of the day, she just wanted him to be happy. And buying the sled for Rio didn't feel selfish. Yes, it *was* about her, but it was a gesture she needed to make. If she could inspire him even a little, they could both be happy.

"I know you want to help your brother," Yvette said carefully. "You can and should. But what do you want?"

"My own business," Nicolette answered promptly. "I want to be famous for really innovative cookie art. And I want to start that non-profit. Maybe one day Rio could inspire others to play."

Her voice was sure and confident, and a tiny bit of relief eased the knots in her stomach. She *did* know what she wanted. She just had to find a way to make it work.

Yvette smiled broadly. "Well, you know we can always set you up here. We'll sell your cookies and you can use the kitchen until you find your own space." Yvette looked around her diner with fond eyes. "You're family. We'll figure it out."

All the emotional upheaval and exhaustion caught up with her, and Nicolette felt her eyes filling. This was the gift she'd always had, people who would do anything for her. It was why she would sacrifice so much for Rio. She wondered why, despite whether what he said was true or not, Matthew couldn't understand that.

"Thank you," she managed, not sure what else would convey her gratitude.

They ate in silence. Thankfully Yvette had brought a carafe of coffee to the table. Between the coffee and the food, Nicolette was starting to feel like a human being again.

Yvette studied Nicolette over the rim of her coffee cup, the steam curling up in soothing spirals.

"Why do I have the feeling there's something else on you mind?"

Nicolette almost denied it. It was all too fresh, her desire for Matthew and her disappointment in him waging desperate war inside her, her confusion an added weapon.

But this was Yvette Ames. If she wanted a real eye on the situation, she could find no one better than this woman. She'd practically raised Matthew along with Austin. She would understand.

"Matthew," Nicolette said, a frustrated frown on her face.

If Yvette was surprised, she didn't show it. Maybe they hadn't been as discreet as she'd thought.

"I wish I could just get rid of my feelings for him, but I can't. I can't give him up." Nicolette heaved a sigh and rubbed her forehead in frustration. "He's so fucking confusing. Half the time, I feel like he's a jerk and not at all the man I thought he was. He is an expert at disappointing me and we argue all the time."

"But?" Yvette pushed.

"But the rest of the time, I would do anything just to make him smile." Nicolette shrugged. "I just want him. I want to be with him. And god, but I want him naked again."

Yvette held up a hand, an awkward chuckle on her lips. "Whoa, girlie, stop right there. I feed that man pot roast every Thursday. I do not need to know what you do with his junk."

Nicolette felt her face warm, but she laughed at Yvette's shocked expression. Parents were hilarious about sex! She knew Yvette had been single a long time, and Austin had never actually known who his dad was, but Nic had a hard time believing the first, last, and only time Yvette had gotten naughty had been when Austin was conceived!

"Sorry," Nicolette said with a chuckle. "He just drives me crazy. In *all* the ways."

Yvette nodded. "I'm glad, though, that you're even considering him. I worry about him. He holds so much of himself back and he's clearly been unhappy."

Nicolette rolled her next question around on her tongue. She wanted to know the truth but was terrified what it would mean.

"Do you know what happened between Rio and Matthew?" she finally asked.

Yvette sighed and set her coffee cup down. "Honey, does it even matter?"

That was not what Nicolette had been expecting. She began to argue but Yvette forged ahead.

"Reality is all about perception," she said sagely. "Whatever you believe to be real is going to be more true than whatever the truth actually is."

Nicolette tried to work this through as Yvette continued.

"As for what happened to them, who knows? They probably don't even remember themselves. But until one of them grows a pair and says I'm sorry, it'll be another decade before anything changes."

Nicolette's heart sank. The likelihood of either man making the first move seemed unlikely at best. Matthew had made his position very clear, and Rio had never even mentioned Matthew until that day in the hospital.

"I think in this case, despite his condition, it's going to have to be Rio who tries first."

Nicolette was taken aback. "Why Rio?"

"Think about it, Nicolette. If Matthew showed up at Rio's bedside and started dredging up old shit, it would make Matthew a monumental asshole. *That* would be putting his own needs before his injured friend's. If Matthew knows he can't visit Rio without putting his baggage aside, he's doing the right thing by staying away."

Shocked, Nicolette stared at Yvette for a few moments. She couldn't believe that she hadn't thought about it that way before. If Matthew went to Rio wanting to hash it out, he'd be adding to Rio's pain, even if his intentions were to heal their friendship.

Clarity dropped into Nicolette's head like a cool drop of water. She knew what she had to do, and it was all thanks to Yvette's wisdom.

"I'll clear this," Nicolette said, practically jumping up from the booth.

"You don't—" Yvette started, but Nicolette was already balancing the plates and cups.

"I'm gonna work another hour if that's okay," she told Yvette, who nodded.

Pausing, Nicolette looked down at Yvette. She had aged a little while Nicolette had been in Denver, had maybe a few more gray hairs sparkling through that same white-blond mane that Austin had. But her open, kind face was the same as that of the woman who had given them slices of pie and cold milk when they visited after hockey games. She'd always remembered Nicolette's birthday and had fed them for weeks when Robin had died.

On a whim, Nicolette leaned down and kissed Yvette's cheek.

The other woman looked surprised but pleased. "What was that for?"

"For being my family," Nicolette answered with a smile.

Yvette's eyes grew a little glossy and she shooed Nicolette away to the kitchen.

She'd left her dough out in her haste to get to breakfast, so she tossed the melty mess and started over.

A funny idea had occurred to her while making the new batch of dough, and she whistled while she hand-cut the shapes and put them in the oven. Mixing the colors into the frosting was always her favorite part, watching the deep pigment swirl into the white. And then she hunched over each cookie, adding the delicate detail.

Once she'd finished, she laid them carefully out on a clean surface and snapped pictures with her phone.

Yvette came up behind her and peered over her shoulder before giggling.

"Oh, Nic, those are adorable!"

Nicolette flushed with pleasure. "Thanks. You can give them to the staff. I got pictures."

Yvette looked aghast. "Oh, no, they're too pretty to eat!"

Nicolette laughed, feeling a little lighter. "They're cookies! You're supposed to eat them. That's the whole point."

With a soft look in her eyes, Yvette squeezed Nicolette's arm. "You're an amazing woman, Nicolette. You know we're proud of you, right? No matter what you do."

Nicolette did know. She knew she wouldn't have made it anywhere without her family holding her up. A part of that family was broken, like a busted tree limb. And she could be the brave one now and make them whole. It would only take a little push.

The breakfast rush was starting up, and Nicolette gathered her things before bidding Yvette goodbye.

"Thank you," she told her.

"For what, honey?" Yvette said with a puzzled smile.

"For everything," Nicolette said, then walked away with a backward wave.

The morning air was cool on her skin and Nicolette breathed deeply for a few moments, tilting her head to soak up the sunshine.

Then she pulled out her phone and sent a quick text to her brother.

Rio, I love you. But I think whatever it takes, you need to make things right with Matthew.

She didn't wait to see if he would respond and silenced her phone. There was nothing else she could say. She had to trust that two stubborn boys could see past their hurt and be happy again.

Because then maybe one of those boys could make her happy, too.

∾

MATTHEW COULDN'T BELIEVE he was here.

He was standing in front of the hospital, clutching two paper cups of coffee. One was black, for him. The other he'd prepared with cream and three sugars.

Just how Rio liked it. Or at least how he'd liked it at eighteen. Maybe he'd grown out of his sugar addiction.

People passing by were shooting him concerned looks. He must look a little crazy, shifting anxiously from foot to foot as the coffee burned his palms. He should have gotten those little cardboard sleeves. But he'd been in a hurry.

He'd sat on the couch all night thinking about Nicolette. Bouncing back and forth from how amazing it had been with her to her barbed words, he'd tortured himself deep into the night. He was an asshole. *She* was an asshole. This was how it would always be and there was nothing he could do about it. It was all Rio's fault he was alone.

On and on, a litany of self-indulgent thoughts, his righteousness tinged with despair.

Somewhere around four in the morning, utterly drained, he dragged himself from the couch and headed to the kitchen for some water. As he sipped, he stood in front of his refrigerator. It was high-end, all gleaming stainless steel, and completely devoid of anything personal. No magnets or pictures of his family. No outdated concert tickets and invitations to weddings long past. He hadn't so much as hung a grocery list.

As he stood there in front of his fridge, the full force of everything he'd lost hit him like a punch to the gut. He hadn't just burned bridges with his family ten years ago. He'd cut himself off from even the possibility of belonging.

Nicolette had fought through that barrier, and he'd done nothing but push her away. She was right. He *was* selfish. And he had not just an empty fridge to show for it. He had an empty life.

A little voice whispered in his tired mind.

What do you want?

The answer to that had changed drastically in the last few weeks. Once it had been to build his business and keep his head down. But now, he just wanted to be the man that Nicolette imagined him to be. To be deserving of her love.

What are you willing to do? the voice urged.

What he should have done a long time ago. Believe that there were people who cared enough about him and it was worth finding a way to forgive. So that he could be with his family, where he belonged.

And here he was, waffling in front of the hospital. What had seemed like bravery at four a.m. now seemed foolish. What would he even say?

As he struggled with his wasted thoughts, his phone buzzed in his pocket. Juggling the coffee cups, he managed to fish it out. The number wasn't in his contacts, but he recognized it immediately. He'd always memorized numbers easily, because his parents never kept the same one long.

Matthew barked a laugh. Rio still had the same damn

number he'd had as a teenager. He'd always been a phone call away.

Matthew read the text.

Hey man. Long time no talk. We need to fix that.

Hardly believing it could be this simple, he quickly replied.

That could be arranged. What did you have in mind?

The answer came back almost instantly.

I'm sure you know what happened to me. I've got a lot of time between appointments. You up for a call sometime?

Matthew grinned and didn't respond, instead stepped through the automatic doors and asked directions to Rio's room.

Rio's room was at the end of a hall, quiet but for the bustle of doctors. The door was slightly ajar. Matthew took a deep breath, rapped on the door, and peered around it.

"Mind face to face instead?"

The sight of Rio after ten years was more shocking than Matthew had anticipated. He was wearing his hair shorter now and had grown into those big ears of his. All normal side effects of growing up.

But the marks of his ordeal were plain. His face was gaunt, a dark beard coming in across his normally clean jaw. He sat hunched slightly, bowed under what must be pain. But the worst thing was his eyes. They were sunken and a little dull. The naughty spark that had lived there was gone, and Matthew felt his heart splitting at seeing the man he'd thought was unbreakable looking so...broken.

Rio sat up as Matthew entered the room, joy erasing some of the fatigue.

"Matthew?" he breathed, like he was seeing a ghost.

"Oh, man," was all Matthew could say, coming to stand at Rio's bedside. Though a blanket covered most of Rio's body, Matthew could only imagine the damage he had suffered. The unseen pain, the bruising and scars. The sight of his larger-than-life friend like this was too much. His throat burned with a rush of emotion, which turned into the sting of tears when Rio was unable to meet his gaze.

Rio was ashamed, Matthew realized with horror. Suddenly, everything clicked into place. All of Nicolette's plans and her determination to push Matthew and Rio back together. Of course she would want to do something, *anything*, to help. He would have done the same, if only he hadn't been a colossal asshole.

But now that he was here, he could try to make it up. He was going to do whatever it took to help Rio find his way.

"I brought coffee," Matthew said roughly, pushing a cup into Rio's hands.

Rio took a sip, then gave a crooked smile. "Oh, Matthew, you old romantic. You remembered how I take it."

"Anyway you find it," Matthew shot back, giddy at how easily they fell back into their rhythm.

Rio chuckled. "Pull up a chair."

Matthew sat and they stared at each other for a few moments, uncertainty heavy in the air between them. Everything about Rio was so familiar and yet unknown. Matthew had so much he wanted to say that he wasn't sure where to start.

"So," Matthew said, picking at the lid of his coffee. "Are they treating you okay here?"

Rio held up a small cylinder with a button on the end. It was attached by a cord to a square machine mounted on the wall.

"All the drugs I can get," he said lightly, but his smile quickly vanished. "But sometimes it's just not enough. It...God, it just really hurts."

Matthew nodded, because he could only imagine. To deal with constant physical pain and to know what it ultimately meant, that his life would never be the same. His career, his passion—his everything. Over. A loss compounded by a loss.

"Rio, I—"

"Don't apologize, if that's what you were gonna say," Rio said gently. "I'm so sick of people apologizing. The accident was caused by a drunk asshole behind the wheel of that car. And I just happened to be sitting in the unlucky spot on the bus. Nicolette likes to remind me that it could have been so much worse."

Rio's words were brave, but Matthew knew his friend. This was the worst thing that Rio could have imagined.

A little of Rio's old spark glinted in his eyes.

"Speaking of Nicolette, what's going on between the two of you?"

Matthew sputtered and began to furiously deny anything, but Rio just laughed.

"You need to take her out, man. Like dinner or a movie or something, while she's in town. She's been in love with you forever." Rio peered at Matthew. "You knew that, right?"

"I mean, I knew she had a crush," Matthew admitted. "But I didn't think it was, like, a thing."

Rio nodded knowingly. "Oh yeah. She pined, my friend. Record-setting levels of pine-age, if I'm being honest."

Matthew bristled slightly at the word honest, but quickly huffed a laugh. "Well, it doesn't really matter. She's not very happy with me right now."

"Dude," Rio said, looking like he was enjoying this way too much. "That's not true. She talks about you constantly. It's cute but also incredibly annoying. Like incredibly..."

Matthew didn't say anything, thinking of their argument. There was no way she would forgive him so easily.

"Listen," Rio said. "If this is a weird protective older-brother thing, I give you my blessing." He waved his hand around in the air like a drunk priest. "Go forth and do your thing. Just don't tell me details. *Ever*."

They chuckled and fell into a surprisingly comfortable silence.

Rio set his coffee cup down on his bedside table and folded his hands in his lap. The IV in his arm brought Matthew back to reality and to why he was here. He opened his mouth to speak but Rio got there first.

"Hey, man, I need to apologize," Rio said in a rush, as if he'd been holding the words in for a while.

"No, no," Matthew desperately protested. "I'm the one that needs to."

Rio ignored him, fixing his eyes on the ceiling as he talked. "You know, I'm not really sure what happened back in the day. You lost your scholarship and I just...I was young, man. I was so turned on by the idea of fame and money. I just couldn't understand why you wouldn't want to go pro with me. I was a shitty friend and I didn't support you when you needed me. You lost your dream. I didn't have a fucking clue what you were going through back then with your parents and all, but I get that now. And I really am fucking sorry."

Matthew found himself blinking like an owl. "What the hell are you talking about?" he burst, unable to tiptoe around the issue anymore. Rio reared back at this outburst, but Matthew barged on. "I don't get you. Why the hell would you want to be supportive when I lost my scholarship if you were the reason I lost it? You were the one who ratted me out to DU. They would never have found out about the financial aid shit if you hadn't said something!"

A look of horror crossed Rio's gaunt face. "You seriously think I did that? I would *never* have done that to you." He was clutching the blanket with white-knuckled fingers, color rising to his cheeks. "Even if I wanted to, I wouldn't have known how! My head was so far up my ass all I could see was pucks in a goal and a long future on the ice. But, Jesus, Matthew. Even if I didn't want you to leave, I wouldn't have done anything to stop you. You actually thought I made a call and got your funds yanked? Your spot on the team pulled? How could you even think that?"

Matthew had expected Rio to deny it, to bullshit his way through. What he hadn't expected was the gray sag of true remorse on Rio's face. It was the look of a man who just realized that he'd been on the wrong end of a very, very bad mistake.

Rio shook his head. "Yeah, I wanted us to stay together. We all knew Austin wasn't good enough to go pro, but you were. I thought we could go travel the world together, brothers on the ice. And then you disappeared."

Matthew sat stunned. He felt like his whole world had tilted on its axis. The anger he'd clung to for so many years had been based in nothing but smoke. He could hardly fathom that the reality he'd clung to, the story that fueled his passion and rage for a decade...was wrong?

He knew he should address all that Rio had said, but there was only one question burning his tongue. "Then how did DU know about my parents?"

There was a new look on Rio's face, one that Matthew had never seen. Compassion.

"My parents only told me this years later and they swore me to secrecy," Rio began. "The IRS had been onto your parents for years. Remember all those extra clothes we kept for you and Shelby and Jackson? All that hockey gear of yours we kept in the van?"

Matthew nodded mutely.

"My mom stockpiled that stuff. She was terrified the IRS

would come and seize everything and you all would be left with nothing."

"She did that?" Matthew asked softly. He knew Robin had cared for him, but this was next level.

"Everybody knew for years your parents homeschooling Shelby was bullshit." Rio said this calmly, plainly. "I mean, your sister never seemed to do anything but tag along with Nic to our practices, you know? All those trips, all the expenses and shit your parents wrote off for your dad's tutoring business and for Shelby's homeschooling? Such a fucking crock."

Matthew's face burned in shame. He wondered who'd really had their head so far up their ass all those years ago. He and Jackson had gone to school, but it was true. Shelby had been homeschooled by their mom, starting in about third grade. Right about the time their dad lost yet another business...and launched a tutoring company. It all seemed to make perfect sense to Matthew as a kid. But adult Matthew could see the truth now that connected the lies. The vacations his parents took, the cars. They even had real estate, which they'd lost in the plea bargain—vacation homes and condos that over the years they'd acquired as tutoring centers or something else. But it came out later that they'd never operated a business out of any of them.

"My mom loved you, man," Rio said, as if this was the most obvious fact in the universe. "A few months before you lost your scholarship, she called a family meeting. She asked me if I would be okay giving my room to you or Jackson or both of you when I went to Italy." He laughed. "I was nineteen and about to go live my dream. I had no idea what she was talking about. Of course I agreed, and I was still holding out that you would come with me so you wouldn't even need the room."

"Why would she ask this?" Matthew truly had no clue. He'd spent so long feeling like he was playing second fiddle, and he'd had so many people on his side. And he'd repaid them by abandoning them.

"Dude, people came by the house. They asked questions, you know? Investigator types. My mom actually was worried that Shelby was going to get taken away or something. We had no idea what was going on, but Mom knew enough to make sure Shelby was with us as often as possible."

Matthew felt nearly sick hearing this. It all made so much sense now. Shelby tagging along with Nic wasn't just because everyone couldn't get enough of the Terrible Trio. The Hayeses had been looking out for Matthew longer than he could have ever known. And he hadn't had the balls to even show up when Robin died.

Rio rolled his eyes. "Stop feeling sorry for yourself, man. It's all over your face. How could you know?" Rio said. "Mom and Dad never talked down about your parents, but they knew that things were going south. They didn't know details. All they cared about was protecting you kids. I never asked questions, what the fuck did I care? You could have moved into my room—I wanted you there. I wanted you in Italy too. Just not enough to steal Denver from you."

"Goddamn," Matthew swore, raking a hand through his hair. "All these years...I always assumed that someone tipped off DU to the scandal and their arrest. It wasn't national news, so I figured there would be no way that DU would have known to look again at my financial aid unless someone called them or tipped them off."

"I don't know, man," Rio said. "You can ask my dad more if you want. There was this ongoing investigation and these dudes in suits would show up at our door asking questions about your parents and their travel expenses. Shit, they even asked about hockey, like who was paying for gear and ice time. I would not doubt at all that the Feds or the IRS or someone asked for copies of the financial aid form to verify the income and shit your parents were claiming. I mean, fraud is fraud, man. Fraud on a federal financial aid form would be some pretty good evidence to use against them, no?"

Matthew swallowed hard, shame coloring his face yet again.

Rio peered at Matthew, trying to catch his eye. "You okay?"

"I don't know," he answered honestly. "All this...it changed my whole life. Everything I thought was wrong. I fucking blamed the wrong people all this time. I mean, my parents, yes, but...you." Matthew rubbed the sting of tears from his eyes. "I'm not sure what to do."

"Did your parents ever explain themselves?" Rio wondered.

Matthew shook his head. "I haven't spoken to them since it happened. Shelby keeps me updated. I know they haven't ended up in jail, but I stopped trying with them. Just like with you. I hid from everyone—just fucking shut everyone out. Like a coward."

"You're not a coward!" Rio declared, and Matthew was shocked to see tears filling his friend's eyes. "I don't know which is worse...losing my career or losing my best friend for ten years because of a dumb misunderstanding." He dashed his tears away with the heels of his hands. "But you are not a coward. You were just a kid with a dream trying to make it. It's not your fault this happened. You didn't know what your parents were doing, and I actually fucking can believe you would think that I had a hand in your losing DU. I probably would have looked for someone like me to blame if I were in your shoes. God knows that would be easier than blaming my own parents."

Silence settled between the men as a nurse came in and took Rio's vitals. The woman made small talk and seemed completely oblivious to the fact that she'd interrupted a tense, emotionally charged conversation. But the break seemed to do the old friends good. By the time the nurse left, Matthew's eyes were dry and Rio had a shit-eating grin on his face.

"I'm not fucking crying over my career, asshole. So I'm sure as hell not crying over you. We all made mistakes, dude. Stop carrying them alone. But I am sorry," Rio said, clearing his throat of emotion. "I'm sorry I was a shitty friend."

Matthew waited for the vindication to come. He waited to feel pity or disgust at himself for not saying those words first. But nothing came, only a curious calm.

Rio was his friend. A real friend. And he was in a world of pain and doubt in a way that probably only Matthew could begin to understand. He was tired of watching the people he loved sacrifice their dreams, and he wouldn't let Rio do it either, no matter how hard it was.

Nicolette would be proud.

And just like that, the key to winning her back clicked into place.

"And?" Rio grumped. "I just bared my soul and I'd love to feel like I'm not the only one all emo and weepy here, shithead."

Sobering, Matthew leaned forward in his chair.

"I was thinking about Nicolette and how stubborn she is. And how she wants you to get better at any cost. I was a shitty friend too, Rio, and I fought her about helping you because of it. But I'm ready now. I want my family back. And I want my brother to be happy and I will help him do that, whatever it takes."

"Fuck, man," Rio sniffled. "Give a guy warning."

"Nah, I'm done with that shit," he said with a grin. "You're now stuck with new Matthew. He's gonna give you a lot more shit and probably some hard truths."

He glanced meaningfully at Rio's feet, and for the first time, Rio shied away.

Matthew's heart ached, wanting to rage against the unfairness of the situation. But he'd learned over ten long years that that solved nothing. So instead he stood, gathered the coffee cups, and looked down at Rio.

"I can't tell you that everything will be okay," Matthew said. "I wouldn't bullshit you. But I know *you* will be. I'll be here to make sure. And I am so, so sorry I ever missed a day of our friendship, man. It will not happen again. I'm sorry."

Rio gave a slight nod before opening his arms for an awkward hug from Matthew.

"Get the fuck out of here, now," Rio said, his head sagging back against the pillows. "I need to press this magic button and get my beauty sleep. I'm going to need to be gorgeous now that none of us assholes are playing hockey."

Matthew grinned and turned off the light as he left the room. As impossible as it seemed, he had Rio back. Now he just had to win back Nicolette.

TEN

Nicolette hunched over the desk in her childhood bedroom. Though years has passed since she'd worked or studied here, the space felt more like home than any place else. She rested her feet on the familiar slats of the worn white wooden chair and contemplated her computer screen. She chewed absent-mindedly on the cap of a pen as ideas swirled through her mind. She was so lost in thought it took a few moments to realize that the noise that was distracting her work was in fact her phone was ringing. She fumbled under sketches and papers that she'd scattered around her searching for the device. She half expected it to be Rhoslyn, calling to check in.

But when she spotted the number on her caller ID, her heart thumped madly in her chest.

All the confidence she'd built up around her seemed to drain away, and she just stared at the screen for a moment. She felt fifteen again. Even with everything that had happened, she still felt that surge of giggly energy seeing his name.

She thumbed the answer button.

"Matthew?" she asked, her voice tellingly breathy.

"Hey," he greeted.

She almost moaned at hearing his voice again, craving any part of him she could get.

"Um, I was notified that you left something at the airport," he said. "I wanted to come get you so we could go claim it."

"Wait, what?" she said, quickly shifting gears. She frantically thought through her belongings and whether she was missing anything. "I don't think I did? And why wouldn't they call me? I mean—"

Matthew chuckled, the sound exasperated and adorable. "Okay, okay, I was not entirely telling the truth. I have something for you and that seemed like a really clever way to ask you out."

She laughed. "You are so weird!"

"Guilty," he said, a smile in his voice.

Nicolette leaned back in her chair and tapped her pen to her lips. "Okay, when is this date happening?"

"Now. I'm already in your house."

Nicolette sat forward. "You're calling me from inside my house? Isn't that what happens in the horror movies?"

"Nicolette, just get your hot ass to the living room."

She couldn't really argue with that, but she took her time going downstairs. She took a quick swing by the bathroom to check her hair in the mirror.

Matthew was standing by the mantle and he turned to face her as she walked down the stairs. The sight of him nearly stopped her in her tracks. Wearing dark jeans, a simple button-down shirt, and a down vest, he looked like a meal. It didn't help that he'd rolled up his sleeves, revealing his corded forearms, or that his hair had been carefully swept back from his forehead.

Her hands itched to touch him, so she crossed her arms to protect him. And herself.

"You know this is breaking and entering, right?" she teased.

He rubbed the back of his neck sheepishly. "Well you told me your dad still kept the spare key in the same old place. I figured I could use it, you know... like the good old days."

"Oh, Dad," Nicolette sighed, but she couldn't seem to stop grinning. *The good old days...* Something about Matthew had changed. He seemed lighter, quicker to smile. She wanted to explore that change, but first she was dying to know where this little "date" was going. "Okay, so now what?" Nic prompted tersely, not ready to let him completely off the hook. Their last words had been in anger and those wounds still stung.

"Basement," Matthew said, his eyes sparkling with excitement. "Your present was too big to hide."

"My present?" she parroted. "I thought we were going out."

"We can, if you want," Matthew said easily. "After you see your present." He held out his hand. "Come on, Nicolette. Let's go on an adventure."

Well, she couldn't refuse that. She let him lead her down the stairs, where the lights were already on. She hadn't been down here in a while, but it was basically the same as it always had been. Blue sectional sofa parked in front of a huge TV. Mom's old crafting table covered in magazines and patterns. Rio's weights in the corner.

"You're right," Nicolette mused, looking at all the yarn still stuffed in a basket by the table. "Dad never changes things. I think the TV is the only new thing."

"He told me he upgraded last year so he could watch Rio in HD," Matthew said with a soft smile. "Come over here."

In the back corner of the basement, something large was draped with the afghan Nicolette had loaned Matthew when he'd spent the night. There was no discerning feature she could make out. She had literally no idea what could be hidden beneath her mom's precious afghan. It just looked like a big multi-colored lump.

"Go ahead," he urged, and she had to laugh at his obvious glee. She pulled the cover away, and her laughter caught in her throat. She covered her mouth with her hand, unable to believe what she was seeing.

A brand-new adaptive hockey sled sat in her basement. This was an even better model than the one she'd been considering buying for Rio—a lighter and more aerodynamic version.

And it was here, waiting for her like a beacon of all her hopes.

"Oh, Matthew, what did you do?" she asked, trying to hold back her tears, but it was no use. They began spilling down her cheeks with a vengeance.

He took one of her hands while using his other one to wipe her tears. "I'm in the process of buying a building. I just used some of my down payment to buy the sled."

"*Just.*" She hiccupped a laugh, and he squeezed her hand.

"I needed to do it, Nic. Now you can figure out what you need for yourself, and no matter what you choose, when Rio goes to rehab, the sled will be there for him. And so will I."

Her breath caught. "You saw him."

Matthew nodded. "I did. It was hard. But we figured it out." A silly grin crossed his face. "He even gave me his blessing to woo you."

"Woo me? His blessing?" Nicolette rolled her eyes. "Men."

She sobered quickly. Though she loved her brother, Matthew knew him better in some ways. "Do you think...do you think he'll be okay?" she asked.

Matthew contemplated it for a moment. The silence made her nervous. She didn't know what she would think if Rio wasn't going to be okay. "I think he needs to want to be," he finally answered. "He has to see past the way things were and get creative about how things could be. I'll help him. And so will you."

"Come upstairs with me," Nicolette demanded suddenly. Her tears had transformed. She was no longer sad. The look she gave Matthew promised gratitude...very lusty displays of gratitude.

Heat flashed in Matthew's eyes. "On a first date, too. Shame, Miss Hayes."

"Not for that," she said, tugging on his hand. Though she was thinking about how he tasted, how hot his skin would be under her hands.... She needed to focus. There was something else she wanted to share with him first. "I have something to show you."

They traipsed up the stairs, back to her childhood bedroom. She'd rehung all of her pictures. The one of the Terrible Trio was framed on her desk. She pulled him over and pointed to the images on her laptop screen. Photo after photo reflected hours of design, baking, and frosting work—all the cookies she'd made at Yvette's.

Matthew peered at her and gave a delighted laugh.

"Nic, those are great!"

She thought so too. She'd made a half a dozen blue hippos, each one hard at work playing a different sport. One clutched a basketball with a look of intense concentration on its face. Another kicked a soccer ball, puffing its cheeks out.

And her favorite, the hockey one, showed the hippo wielding a stick far too small for its rotund frame.

"It's part of my new portfolio," she explained, minimizing the photos to show him the website pulled up behind them. "I'm applying for next year's comic con. The Chicago con. I missed the cutoff for this year," she explained, "but that will give me even more time to prepare. Blue Hippo is going to be there, but there are other vendors who might like my work and—"

Nicolette was cut off with an "Oof!" as Matthew pulled her against him, wrapping her in his arms.

"I'll figure my way, Matthew," she whispered into his chest. "I won't give up my dream. But I belong here. With my dad and Rio. And you."

He leaned back a little, staring down at her with so much tenderness she wanted to pop.

"Well, that building I'm buying? It has a lower level that is zoned for food service. I was thinking about putting in a commercial kitchen. We're about six months away, but who knows? There might just be a spot for a clever baker with no credit or income."

"Matthew," Nicolette whispered, overwhelmed by his generosity. She'd always known this was him; she'd just never been on the receiving end of it. It was almost too much to take in.

"Shelby is coming home on summer break and might need a summer job," Matthew mused. "Though if she's involved in some marketing internship, there's her roommate. She's been working at a pizza place and knows her way around dough. Maybe she'll be interested in working with a famous cookie artist."

"You have everything figured out, don't you?" Nicolette said, leaning back in his arms to look at him.

"It's how I've survived," he said, and though his tone was light, the history there was plain as day.

"I'm sorry," she whispered, laying her head against his chest.

"What for?" he said, his voice a rumble against her cheek.

"For all those awful things I said. Rio told me everything that happened with your parents and...Matthew, I'm just so sorry."

"Me too," he said, stroking her hair. "I was a total dick. And

I was as selfish as you said. You saw right through me, and you gave me the stick to the nuts that I needed."

"Matthew," she laughed. "I take it you're feeling more open to hockey? Are we going for full analogies now, or is it too soon?"

He cracked a self-conscious smile. "You don't need to protect me anymore—form anything. Because of you I've been able to see myself for the first time in ages. I don't have to be tied down by my past anymore. I have my brother back and I can help him. I don't know what role if any hockey will have in my future, but it doesn't have to be the monster under the bed anymore. You know? And now I have this amazing woman who is smart, and hilarious, and talented, and whom I really want to kiss."

Nicolette grabbed his face and reached up to kiss him, having to strain on tiptoes. Matthew's eyes fluttered closed like he was feeling relief from pain, and he kissed her back, sweet slow kisses, just a gentle press of their mouths together.

It was heavenly, just being close to him, surrounded by his warm scent. But she wanted more, needed to be closer. So after gently angling his body, she pushed him down on her bed before scrambling into his lap.

"Impatient, are we?" he asked, then nipped at her lip playfully, before soothing the sting with his tongue.

"We've wasted a lot of time," she gasped as he moved his hands up her sides, just cresting the curve of her breast.

"But now we have all the time in the world," he said, and finally he kissed her like she wanted, taking her mouth with a clever tongue and soft lips.

She held on to him for dear life, the feel of the muscles sliding under his skin so delightfully erotic that she wanted more. Breaking the kiss, she nudged him and his back hit her headboard.

"Ouch!" he exclaimed.

Nicolette covered her mouth in mortification, and then waddled forward on her knees until she was at his side.

"I'm so sorry! Did you hit your head?"

"No." He grimaced. "There's something..." He reached under his hip and produced a sketchbook, the hardcover kind she'd preferred as a teenager. It was the same one Matthew had found when he'd spent the night, with the drawing of him in hockey gear.

He glanced at her, nudging the cover with his thumb. "Can I?"

Fifteen-year-old Nicolette was screaming *NO!*, but she hadn't known Matthew then. Not really. This Matthew she trusted.

"Go ahead," she said, settling next to him.

He started flipping through, and Nicolette cringed at how amateurish her art looked. There were drawings of her parents and her friends, and the only dog they'd ever had, Cobalt. Things a kid would draw.

Toward the middle of the book, where they could be hidden from the casual snooper, were Nicolette's hockey drawings. Yes, there were a few of her brother and Austin, or the three of them. But it was mostly Matthew.

Matthew looking focused on the bench. Matthew celebrating after a goal. Matthew standing facing away from her during the national anthem, number twenty proudly displayed along with his name.

"You really did like me," he mused.

"I did like you," she said, taking the sketchbook from his hands and setting it aside. "But I didn't really know you. Now that I do, I love you."

He stared at her, a thousand things flickering across his gaze and all of them beautiful.

"I love you," he said with a little bit of wonder in his tone. "I'll do whatever it takes to deserve you, Nicolette."

She climbed back into his lap, straddling his hips. "Matthew, you already do. And I think it's okay to take some things that are just for you. You've given so much. Let me support you too."

His kiss was desperate and tender, a soft invasion building to unbearable heat. His hands were everywhere, in her hair, on her shoulders, grabbing her ass. Each touch was a brand, tying them more firmly together.

Cool air teased her skin as Matthew helped her pull her shirt over her head. He attacked her exposed skin, dragging his teeth across her collarbone until she was moaning his name. He answered with his own grunt, pushing his hips so he rubbed against her.

"Shirt off," she breathed, and he complied, before reclaiming her mouth. She let her hands roam then, marveling at the ridges of muscle that seemed to be everywhere on his body.

Matthew reached around to unhook her bra, but then froze suddenly.

"What is it?" she asked, alarmed.

"When does your dad get home from work?" Matthew asked in a panic.

After a stunned pause, Nicolette began to laugh, great heaving giggles. She had to rest her head against Matthew's chest as she continued to shake with mirth.

"What?" he asked, sounding a little defensive.

She wiped her eyes and pressed a small kiss to his lips.

"You're what, six foot four?"

He nodded.

"Two hundred pounds?"

"Give or take," he said, now seeming to get her drift.

"Yeah, my dad's a pasty old dude. The worst he'll do is give you an awkward talk about not hurting me."

Matthew shuddered. "From Keith? That sounds like a nightmare."

Nicolette shrugged and removed her bra, distracting Matthew the best way she knew how. She grabbed his hands and placed them on her, his skin so warm that she felt the echoing warmth in her core.

"Well," she managed as he began to stroke and tease her. "If you want to avoid Dad altogether, you'd better make this quick and dirty, huh?"

He paused, his desire-dark eyes meeting hers with purpose.

"Nothing about you is quick and dirty, Nicolette," he said. "I lost ten years. I'm gonna take my time and focus on all the details. Just like decorating cookies, right?"

Nicolette ran a hand over his face, and he leaned into it.

"I think you're onto something," she said.

Matthew slid a hand beneath Nic's hair so he could angle her face to his. He kissed her once for every year they'd missed, for all the misunderstandings and the losses. He kissed her with the promise of everything that was yet to come. "I love you, babe," he breathed. "A love story ten years in the making, the perfect family, and a brotherhood that got fixed just in time," he said.

With a growl, Matthew took a gentle handful of Nic's hair and pulled her in for a blistering kiss. She moaned into his mouth, and he used the opportunity to slide his tongue against hers, causing her to rock her hips against his hardening cock.

"Nicolette," Matthew moaned, low and guttural. He skated his free hand down her back, coming to rest on her ass. Grabbing a healthy palmful, he pressed her more firmly against his body.

Nicolette wanted to throw her head back and just *feel*. The heat from Matthew's body was searing even through her jeans, and his cock pressed against her in just the right way. His slow movements against her were maddening and delicious, each thrust sending her pulse skittering.

But when Matthew broke their kiss, Nicolette found she couldn't tear her eyes from his. They were filled with lust and tenderness and no small amount of vulnerability. Though they'd said 'I love you,' it wasn't until that moment that Nicolette realized he was trusting her with his heart.

Nicolette slowed her movements to a stop and reached for Matthew's hand. His puzzled look melted away when Nicolette placed his palm over her left breast. Holding his wrist there for a few moments, Nicolette hoped he could feel how excited she was, and how hopeful. For him. For them.

A small smile tugged the corner of Matthew's mouth and he squeezed her breast.

"All the details, right, Nic?" he whispered, his squeeze turning into a caress.

She leaned into his touch like a lazy cat. "Yes," she panted. "And maybe the big detail in your pants."

Matthew guffawed, the sound snaking through Nic's body like quicksilver. "You're going to have to help me with that," he said, waggling his eyebrows. "This bed is, um, smaller than I'm used to."

Nicolette giggled. Matthew's huge body on her twin sized bed did present a challenge. His broad shoulders spanned almost the full width of her headboard. This was a challenge she was willing to take.

She supposed it should be a little weird to be having sex with her childhood crush in her childhood bed. She was surrounded by all the trappings of home and family, everything a reflection of her dreams and goals. Hardly the stuff of sexy fantasies.

"Do you think it's creepy?" Nicolette asked Matthew as she trailed a hand lazily down his chest.

"Is what creepy?" he grunted, watching intently as Nic flicked open the button on his jeans and dragged his fly down.

"Being here in this bed," she said, sliding her fingertips under the waistband if his boxer-briefs. "Where I may or may not have had dirty fantasies about you."

Matthew groaned as she skated her hand over his cock.

"It's not creepy," he gritted as she lightly teased him. "It just means that some dreams come true."

Nicolette leaned down and kissed him softly. Matthew would understand. Every detail in this room was a mile marker on the road to this moment, to this man. He knew what it meant to be defined by the past, and how much it meant to overcome it. Their coming together here made sense.

God, just when she thought she couldn't love him more, he proved to be the man she'd always recognized him to be.

"Nic," Matthew begged between her light kisses and caresses. "While I do want to take it slow..."

"Less pants?" she asked and placed a kiss on his stubbly chin.

He huffed a laugh. "You know how to sweet talk a man."

Scooching off his legs, she pulled his jeans and underwear down as he wriggled out of them. Nicolette tossed the garments aside and removed her own until there was nothing between them but electrically charged air.

Matthew was still propped up against the headboard, his long limbs stretched out on the bedspread in a mouthwatering display. Nicolette let her eyes roam as she pleased, lingering on the curves of his biceps and his lickable abs. His cock was jutting up between his strong thighs and Nicolette's core clenched involuntarily, remembering what it felt like to have him there.

"Nicolette?" Matthew asked, raising an eyebrow at her. "What's up?"

She shook her head. Only Matthew would be blind to the fact that she was eye-fucking him. She was going to have to work on stoking his ego. Starting now.

"I was staring at the beautiful man I'm about to defile," she answered. "Who doesn't seem to realize how beautiful and defile-able he is."

A hint of red crested Matthew's cheeks. "That's not a word."

"Fight me," Nicolette challenged with a defiant jut of her chin. "You'll lose."

"I know," Matthew said softly, reaching out to stroke her stomach. "I'm already lost."

"Matthew," Nicolette whispered. She wished she had something more to say, better words to let him know that she loved him so much it hurt. The squeezing of her heart along with the intense pangs of desire made her sway on her feet.

Matthew steadied her with a hand on her waist. Nicolette knew he would always be there to catch her.

"Um, condom," she said shakily, groping for the bed side table drawer.

Matthew looked uncertain as she pulled the unopened box from the drawer.

"How long have those been here?" he asked as she pulled the carboard tab open.

Nicolette giggled. "Since I brought Oliver Macy up here senior year for some extracurricular activity."

Matthew wrinkled his nose. "Macy? That meathead?" He shook his head, incredulous. "So not your type."

Nicolette tore open the condom and rolled it gently down Matthew's length. "You're right, he wasn't, which was why he was never here and why I bought new condoms last week in the hopes you would be."

The grin that grew on Matthew's face would have illuminated a cave. Nicolette was so dazzled by it that she was taken by surprise when Matthew grabbed her. He pulled her across his body, so they were chest to chest and nose-to-nose.

He kissed her softly, his lips just grazing hers. "Take that, Oliver Macy," he whispered against her mouth.

Nicolette's laugh was smothered by another kiss, this one deeper. His stubble scraped the sensitive skin around her mouth as he moved under her. The slide of his tongue against hers sent hot pleasure snaking down her body, coming to a throbbing halt between her legs.

A whimper escaped Nicolette's lips as she ground down on Matthew's leg in a desperate attempt to create friction against her swollen clit. Matthew gasped, digging his fingers into the backs of her thighs. His heaving chest pressed against hers, chafing her sensitive nipples in the most delightful way.

"Matthew," she begged, all caution thrown to the wind. She wanted him and she wanted him now. By the glazed look in his eyes and the press of his cock against her stomach, she knew he wasn't too far behind.

"I got you," Matthew whispered, and Nicolette's breath caught in her throat. This echo of their first time together in his condo was almost too much. She wanted to tell him that she had him too. They were in this together now. No more clinging to solitude and uncertainty. She would bring the color and he could bring the strength.

Nic opened her mouth, ready to make an ass of herself to make him understand. But then Matthew rolled her on her side and his hand was between her legs. As his thumb stroked her clit, her words disappeared on a moan. The assurances could wait.

Their stuttered breaths mingled in the small space between their mouths as Matthew slid a finger inside Nicolette. He started an easy rhythm, his free hand wandering her neck, shoulders, and arms.

Nicolette groped for Matthew's cock, wanting to make him feel as good as she felt, but he batted her hand away.

"No," he panted. "Want to see you come."

Without waiting for her argument, he added another finger. All powers of speech abandoned Nicolette. Throwing her head back, she rode Matthew's hand. He pressed light kisses along her jaw and up her neck, murmuring dirty secrets in her ear until Nicolette couldn't stand it anymore. Her body pulled in tight, a diamond of pleasure forming sharp and brilliant in her belly.

"Matthew," she sobbed, scoring his shoulders with desperate fingers.

"I got you," he murmured in her ear, sending Nicolette over the edge with just the warmth in his voice.

Trying to catch her breath, Nicolette pressed her forehead against Matthew's collarbone. He pulled her in close and kissed the top of her head. They lay in companionable silence for a few minutes. Nicolette almost dozed off, until she shifted her leg against Matthew's cock, still rigid in its rubber sheath.

"Matthew," Nicolette scolded. "We should probably take care of that."

"Mmm," he responded noncommittally, as if there was no raging hard on taking up space between them. "It can wait."

She poked him. "And waste the condom?"

He snorted. "Well, when you put it that way..."

Nicolette tilted her head up to kiss him. "Tell me what you want."

She felt him pull back slightly. "I don't—"

"Matthew," Nic said firmly, taking his face between her hands. "I want to know what you want."

He studied her face, his eyes flickering back and forth. A small smile turned up the corner of his mouth and he rolled away from her to rest on his back.

"All right, cowgirl," he drawled, bringing his arm behind his head. "I think you know what to do."

Nicolette scrambled eagerly onto his lap, straddling his lean hips. Matthew's self-satisfied smile drained away when she reached down to stroke his balls, while she rubbed herself up and down his shaft.

"Shit," he grunted, grabbing hold of her hips. "Don't tease, or I'm gonna come."

"Good," Nicolette said, trailing her free hand down her stomach until she reached her clit.

"Oh God," Matthew said hoarsely as she started to play with herself. "Nic, you're beautiful."

Nicolette had never been overly hung up on her looks. She enjoyed her flashy clothes and glasses but never sought to hide behind them. Being naked here with Matthew, she thought that maybe she *had* been hiding a little. But Matthew saw the real Nicolette and thought she was beautiful. And Nic believed him.

Now to make him feel her gratitude. Abandoning her ministrations on her clit, Nicolette reached down and lined Matthew up to her center. She watched with fascination as the tendons in Matthew's neck rose in sharp relief as she lowered herself onto him.

"Nicolette," he managed, his grip on her hips almost bruising. "God, you feel so good. I—"

"Shhh," Nicolette hushed. "Just turn that big brain off for a minute and let this cowgirl work her magic."

Without giving him an opportunity to respond, Nicolette

rose up on her knees. Starting a quick pace, she took him as deep as she could. The slide of his cock against her slick walls was almost too much and she wondered how long she would be able to last.

Matthew was panting beneath her, looking like some pornographic marble statue, all angles and planes. He still held her hips, rocking his own to meet her.

"Touch me," Nicolette demanded. She wanted to feel those big hands everywhere and get as close to him as possible.

Matthew complied, one hand splaying on her stomach, the other heading immediately to her clit.

Nicolette cried out as he stroked her. She threw her head back and squeezed her eyes shut. Fierce bliss suffused her body and she tried to fight the crest of her pleasure, wanting to feel his delicious body against hers for as long as possible.

"Nicolette," Matthew's voice came, a low warning.

She cracked her eyes and found him watching her. His face burned bright with desire and she whimpered at the stroke of lust that snaked through her core.

"Don't close your eyes," Mathew demanded.

Unable to speak, Nicolette nodded. She kept her eyes locked on his even as he began an earnest campaign on her clit, stroking her in time with her movements.

Their movements became frenzied, and Nicolette's core tightened, making each slide of Matthew's cock feel even better. She bore down on him, her climax seeming to build higher and higher without breaking.

"Matthew," she sobbed, breathless with ecstasy.

He responded in kind, with rough thrusts and gentle strokes of her clit until Nic was crying out. Everything tightened into a single point before rushing back out, each nerve suffused with pleasure so sweet it was almost painful.

Nicolette had barely recovered when she was on her back,

Matthew moving between her legs. Nicolette wrapped herself around him, holding him close as he sought his own climax.

She felt every moment of his orgasm. His muscles bunched under her hands, his thrusts grew uneven, and his low cry made her feel just as happy as her own climax had.

Matthew panted above her for a few moments before rolling them onto their sides. Then they were quiet, Matthew playing with a strand of Nicolette's hair as he stole kisses.

"Did that live up to your fantasies?" Matthew rumbled, stroking his knuckles along the side of Nicolette's breast. "How did I compare to Oliver Macy?"

Nicolette huffed a laugh. "I never really thought about Oliver. But you...well, trust me when I say the real you could kick fantasy Matthew's ass."

He chuckled, pleasure crinkling the corner of his eyes. "Nic, I wish I hadn't been such an idiot."

Nicolette ran her hair through his sprinkling of chest hair. "Yes, you're an idiot, but what are you talking about?"

Matthew pinched her side, swiftly tempering the sting with a soft stroke. "I should have seen you. I should have known you were for me. I never would have let you go."

"Well, you have me now," Nicolette assured, tangling her fingers with his.

Instead of looking pleased, Matthew frowned. "Yeah..."

He seemed to turn inward for a moment, his eyes studying a spot somewhere over her shoulder.

"Matthew?" Nicolette asked, growing concerned.

His gaze snapped back to her, intense and intent. "Move in with me," he suddenly demanded.

"What?" Nicolette blurted too fast.

But Matthew didn't seem to notice. He grabbed her shoulder, stroking a thumb along her collar bone.

"Move in with me, Nic. You wouldn't have to worry about

anything. You could use the kitchen at my new building like we talked about and build your business. I'll even drive you to Denver to get your stuff."

"Matthew—" Nicolette tried but he forged ahead.

"I want to move forward," he said, pressing his forehead to hers. "And I think I need you to help me. I want you with me, Nic. I can't let you go. I want to take care of you."

Nicolette stared into his eyes, eyes that had always been so dear to her. He was offering her all she'd ever wanted. This was more than physical. He wanted to share his life with her.

She should say yes. That is what old Nicolette would have done. And the love she felt for this man was certainly pushing her to agree. Maybe being taken care of for once wouldn't be so bad.

So when she finally opened her mouth to answer, Nicolette was half-surprised to hear herself say, "No."

～

"NO."

The word ricocheted through Matthew's skull like a bullet. Just that single syllable had all of Matthew's newfound confidence faltering. He untangled his limbs from Nicolette's and then rose to his feet. The bullet seemed to travel from his head and lodge firmly in his chest.

He stood uncertainly by the bed, gazing down at this maddening and miraculous girl. He'd finally accepted that she was the real thing, something he could trust. Damn it, they'd just had the rawest, most connected sex he'd ever experienced. He'd let her see all the broken parts of him and she'd seemed to accept them. But after all they'd been through, and she still was out of his reach.

Searching her eyes, he tried to find any sign of humor. As if she was suddenly going to shout 'surprise!' and tell him she wanted him as much as he wanted her.

But her gaze was clear and steady. She was certain about him, and nothing he could do would change that. That certainty was one of the things he loved about her. He'd never dreamed that he would hate to be on the receiving end of it.

Once he'd been so adept at hiding his feelings. But Nicolette had weakened his defenses. He could feel his face morphing into a mask of disappointment, his body seeming to bow under the strain.

Concern flickered on Nicolette's face, and she pulled herself to a sitting position.

"Matthew," she said, reaching out for him. "I don't—"

"I have to go to the bathroom," he blurted, before turning tail and bolting from the room.

The bathroom that Nic and Rio shared growing up was painted daffodil yellow. Rio had always grumbled that it was 'too girly.' This was made worse when, in the midst of a mermaid fascination, fourteen-year-old Nic had stenciled a parade of mermaids around the mirror, each one unique.

Though outwardly agreeing with Rio that the mermaids were embarrassing, Matthew had always been fascinated by them. He'd study them, looking for the little details Nic had imbued them with. One was eating bon bons from a tiny box of chocolates. Still another was curled up asleep in a shell with a sleep mask. His favorite was the pink-haired beauty with a pet fish on a leash.

Standing at the sink intending to splash cold water on his face, Matthew let his eyes wander the familiar drawings, looking for some kind of guidance. Maybe one of those mermaids would blink to life and tell him what to do.

"Get your act together!" one would most likely scold. "Nicolette deserves the best."

"I know," Mathew replied, startled by his own voice. He desperately hoped that Keith wasn't lurking somewhere in the house. How would it look if Nic's dad found Matthew stark naked and talking to a mermaid? Certifiable.

Matthew sighed, and turned the squeaky faucet on. The water was ice cold and he welcomed the sting as he splashed his face and neck. The effort brought him no relief.

He wasn't sure what he should do now. His instinct was to run. Let the idea of him and Nic die and go back to the way he was used to living. Yes, he'd been miserable. But the thought that Nic didn't really want him was more painful than any existence he could now imagine.

Of course, his clothes were in Nic's room. He'd have to go back and face her either way. But he wasn't sure he could stomach what she had to say.

"Got any more pearls of wisdom?" he murmured to the mermaids, but they just stared back, mute as to their creator's intentions.

Matthew dried his face and left the bathroom. Standing naked in the hallway, he felt unmoored in this familiar house. This family had been a part of his life for so long. He wondered if, finally, he'd outstayed his welcome.

A sliver of light crept across the carpet toward his feet. It was coming from Rio's room, the cracked door just allowing the hint of afternoon light between the curtains.

Matthew padded to the room and pushed the door open with a creak. Rio would be equal parts amused and horrified if he knew that Matthew was here with his dick hanging out. But Matthew couldn't help but wander in.

Among Rio's trophies and treasures, Matthew felt his defenses clicking back into place. This had been his life for so long. He'd belonged here. And then he hadn't. He wasn't sure where he stood now.

He clenched his fists in a flare of anger. Hadn't he done the right thing? He was putting aside his fears and trusting in Nicolette. He'd seen the way to forgive Rio, not to mention to forgive himself.

"What am I still doing wrong?" he asked the room.

Nothing answered but the tick of the clock atop Rio's bookshelf.

Matthew walked over and pulled a book at random from the shelf. *Moby Dick*. Matthew had to laugh. Rio and his beloved classics.

"Clever asshole," Matthew muttered, flipping through the hefty tome. Matthew had never read this one but recalled Rio raving about it.

"Ahab is never able to let go," Rio had gushed. "He can't take advice and it leads him and everyone around him to a pretty heinous death."

Matthew paused, tracing the terrifying-looking whale that adorned the cover. He didn't think he was as crazy as Captain Ahab. But Matthew had believed with a single-minded intensity in Rio's betrayal. That one action steered his life to the point of blindness to any other way. His tunnel vision had taken him away from hockey—something he'd dedicated his entire childhood to. Away from the Hayes family—even when they probably could have used his support.

And then Nic... Matthew wondered vaguely what might have been. If he'd never bolted and run away, could he and Nic have found their way to each other sooner? Maybe she would never have gone to Denver. *Denver*... The thought occurred to Matthew just now for the first time. Why did she pick that city of all the cities in the world to move to for culinary school? Maybe it seemed crazy, but was it possible that even unconsciously Nic had gone where she knew Matthew had wanted to be? Had she always tried to stay in his orbit? Maybe Matthew wasn't crazy, but he certainly had been a stubborn ass. Whether he was crazy or not, he knew one thing. And that realization changed everything.

His head shot up, and he shoved the book back on the shelf. A small flicker of hope kindled in his chest. His bullheadedness had gotten him into trouble with Nicolette before. Maybe, if he actually listened to her, he'd get the answers he needed. No more running away. This time, he was going to be different.

Matthew slipped back into Nicolette's room and his heart stuttered when he saw her. She was sitting up on the bed, her arms wrapped around her knees. A frown marred her features, and she looked up at him with uncertain eyes.

He sunk down next to her, brushing a stray lock of hair from her forehead. Taking her face in his hands, he kissed her gently.

"Okay," he said, leaning back to look at her. "So what does no mean exactly?"

A little smile quirked the corner of her mouth and eased some of Matthew's tension.

"It means, Matty, that I don't want to move in with you at this moment."

Matthew grimaced. "I hate it when people shorten my name."

Nicolette laughed, the tinkling sound making Matthew's cock twitch. "I know," she said, nudging him with her shoulder. "That's why I said it. You deserve it for running off like that."

"Fair enough," he said and kissed her shoulder. "So you don't want to live with me. Do you want to be with me?"

She looked aghast. "Is that what you thought? That I was breaking up with you?"

Matthew shrugged, trying to look nonchalant. "You did just drop a *no* bomb with no explanation."

Nicolette sighed. "Matthew, when I said I love you, I meant it. It's just..." She hesitated.

"Go ahead," Matthew prompted.

"You have trouble seeing things outside of what you want," she said quickly, as if ripping a Band Aid off. "You try to control every situation, and I think it's so you won't get hurt."

He wanted to deny it, but he couldn't, so he kept quiet.

"I want to be with you," Nicolette went on, placing a hand on his chest. "You'd be scared if you knew how much I want you. But the reason I came here was to help Rio and my dad. I want to be able to have a life and grow my business on my own terms. And I don't think I could do that if I was in your bed twenty-four hours a day."

She smiled tentatively at him, and he took the cue from her joke.

"You're right," he conceded. "That is exactly where I would keep you." He pushed her back onto the bed and settled between her legs. "Your dreams of being a famous cookie artist would go up in a lust-filled haze."

She gave a hearty laugh, drawing his attention to her breasts. But before he could forget himself in her body, she fixed him with a stern look.

"Listen to me, Matthew Collins," she said. "I *will* be a famous cookie artist, and you *will* be my trophy boyfriend, because we deserve it." She ran her hand down his back and grabbed his ass. "We waited too long because we were both too scared to change. But I need you to trust the change and trust me. Everything in its time. Today, we're okay. This is all okay."

Matthew studied her lovely face before leaning down for a tender kiss.

"I do trust you," he whispered against her mouth. "More than I've ever trusted anything. And if that means sneaking into that window to have sex while your dad is down the hall, then that's fine with me."

"Man, do you know how to kill a mood," Nicolette huffed.

"More than that stuffed macaron with googly eyes over there who's staring at my ass?" Matthew grumbled.

Nicolette grabbed the stuffed cookie off of her nightstand and threw it across the room.

"There," she said, wrapping her legs firmly around his hips. "Now there is nothing to come between us being together. Just remember that cutesy cookies are my claim to fame!"

"I wouldn't have you any other way," Matthew sighed.

Chase your Famous!

CHEESE
FAMOUS

A FAMOUS ROMANCE NOVEL

CALLIE CHASE

CONTINUE THE FAMOUS SERIES WITH
CHEESE FAMOUS

If you were at all curious about the movie John was watching in *Pizza Famous*, check out this excerpt from *Cheese Famous*... Child star Tommy Dee is all grown up. And he has secrets that are about to be revealed.

Cheese Famous

Early Spring 2020

"Dunny!"

Duncan Lewis followed the sound of his name being called through the crowded sorority house.

"Dunny!"

"I'm coming!" Duncan nudged past women in tank tops and micro-miniskirts and guys in what seemed to be the uniform for Welcome Back week events: golf shirts and knee-length cargo shorts. Finding his best friend Rayan should have been easy: Duncan looked for the only college kid in the house wearing crisp chambray and impeccably cuffed seersucker trousers. "Ray?" Duncan scratched his beard and peered through the sea of well-curled ponytails and embroidered baseball caps.

Duncan found Rayan far below eye level, sitting in the center seat on a crowded couch, directly opposite the large screen TV. A football game blared in the background, the shrill whistle and droning voices of the commentators adding to the general murmur of conversation of the crowded Saturday afternoon open house. The windows were open and the faint smell of smoke from a charcoal grill wafted in on the late summer breeze. The electronic beats of bass-heavy dance music blasting from a stereo competed with the game. Even though the party had only started a couple of hours ago, a group of girls juggled red plastic cups while they tried to get the karaoke machine working.

Rayan motioned with an arm for Duncan to join him.

"You don't look like you need me," Duncan muttered, a grin on his face. Rayan was surrounded on both sides by tan, attractive women. "I, uh, actually don't think I'll fit, man." Duncan made a rubbing motion over his belly with a freckled hand. While Rayan was well-dressed, well-toned, and well-groomed, Duncan's style was more *everyman*—meaning, just about every man in the room had a better body than he did.

"Oh, but I do," Ryan stood up slowly, smoothing his pants into place. "I am in desperate need of refreshment and I need you to secure my space."

"You don't trust *me* to grab snacks?" Duncan asked, rubbing the back of his wrist across the sweat already collecting on his brow. "Man, I'm literally the cook at our house."

"It's not that," Rayan said in a low voice as he tugged on Duncan's arm. "I need to use the facilities and did not want to give up this prime seat. Save my space," he urged. Rayan nudged Duncan toward the space he'd vacated between two girls on a small sofa. Both women scooched over to make room for Duncan's fuller frame. "Ladies," Rayan addressed the girls immediately on either side of Duncan. "Keep my friend company until I'm back. I promise to return with a cheese plate!"

"That guy," one girl called crooned, shaking her head. "A voice like a British prince and talks about cheese plates. Definitely not your average college student." She flushed. "He's really cool."

"Yeah," Duncan nodded, "he's good people." He reached an arm across his body and shook her hand, frustrated that he was already uncomfortably hot. Even after three years in Chicago, he was not used to midwestern humidity. "Nice to meet you, I'm Duncan," he said.

"Alexis," she said distractedly, her eyes still following Rayan's retreating form.

Duncan turned to the girl to his right, shifting his shoulders in the snug space. "And you're..." he started. He trailed off as he took in the girl beside him.

She stared at him with intense gold-brown eyes. Disapproval twisted her lips into a frown. She clutched the end of her long sandy blonde braid between two fingers.

Duncan was filled with the immediate and unwelcome feeling that he knew this woman... He just couldn't remember from where. He didn't have this experience often anymore, especially since leaving LA. He'd been able to blend easily among the other out-of-shape college dudes in beer T-shirts for so long now, he'd almost forgotten what it was like to be recognized—and to recognize people in the industry. The slight beer paunch that matched his T-shirt helped mask who he was, who he used to be. The extra weight matured him in a way that made him blissfully unrecognizable most of the time. The beard he'd carefully cultivated since puberty covered up his face creating an almost iron-clad disguise: adulthood. While most college guys probably tried to stand out, Duncan tried to blend in. He had reasons for that. But this girl's pinched mouth and laser-sharp squint was familiar. Too familiar.

There's no way I know her, he reassured himself. *And she doesn't know me.*

He took a steadying breath and reminded himself to play it cool. "Your name is?" he asked.

"As if you don't know," she scoffed. She gave him an impatient look, one brow quirked in irritation. "Bree," she finally supplied. She might as well have rolled her eyes and smacked him.

"That's a really beautiful name," he said politely, hoping he still had sufficient acting skills to appear calm despite the tendrils of panic that scratched along the back of his neck.

Fuck. Bree. Her searched his memory banks but came up empty. *That's a rare enough name that...*

"I know you," she said quietly. She didn't take his outstretched hand, but looked at it as though she disliked his fingers intensely. "We know each other," she corrected.

Duncan fell immediately into character. He'd been down this road before. This was a role he could still play. "No, no, I don't think so." He put on a huge smile and looked right in her eyes. Making eye contact always helped the lies feel more true. "I'd remember someone with your name, I'm sure. But nice to meet you."

He turned his attention back to Alexis who was asking how Duncan knew Rayan. "He's my housemate, my roommate," he explained. "He's one of my oldest friends."

"He's not, really." Bree challenged him, squinting at him.

Duncan felt the sting of her electric glare before he shifted to look at her. Alexis seemed blissfully unable to hear their exchange, her focus back on searching the crowd while she waited for Rayan to return.

"Look, uh, Bree," Duncan started. "I really don't think—"

Bree held a hand up and pressed a single finger to Duncan's shoulder. She leaned close to him, the heat from her smooth arm burning through the sleeve of his worn out T-shirt.

"I know it's you." He closed his eyes as her fragrance, something sweet like cookies, teased his nose. She brought her lips to his ear and whispered his stage name in a low, menacing voice. *"Tommy."*

Continue Reading

ALSO BY CALLIE CHASE

Famous Series:

Mistletoe Famous

Pizza Famous

Cookie Famous

Cheese Famous (coming soon)

Food Infamous (coming soon)

Hockey Famous (coming 2020)

Royal Famous (coming 2020)

ALSO FROM PINK SAND PRESS

Marci Bolden

Stonehill Series

The Road Leads Back

Friends Without Benefits

The Forgotten Path

Jessica's Wish

This Old Cafe

Forever Yours

Standalones

California Can Wait

Seducing Kate

The Rebound

ACKNOWLEDGMENTS

The author would like to thank these wonderful, talented people for their hard work and sugar-sweet devotion to Nic, Matthew, Rio, and *Cookie Famous*:

Jeanne De Vita
Ann Marie Mori
Rachel Rozdzial

Everyone else on the team at Pink Sand Press (y'all rock!), the Tessera Editorial team, including Christa Desir and Isabel Ngo, as well as Yasmin McClinton, RaeChell Garrett, and Renae Moore, as well as special thanks to Laura Scott.

9 781950 348374